ELLE GRAY | K.S. GRAY

OLIVIA KNIGHT

FBI MYSTERY THRILLER

FATAL LIES

Fatal Lies
Copyright © 2024 by Elle Gray | K.S. Gray

CHAPTER ONE

"**H**ELLO," ADELINE CLARKE SAID, GRINNING. "HAVE you missed me?"

Olivia stared at the screen of the phone in front of her in horror. She was still standing outside the church where her cousin's funeral had taken place, faced with a mysterious man in the graveyard and a familiar old face on Facetime. The Gamemaster had long been a thorn in their sides now, but Olivia had a feeling that this was the last time she would face their nemesis. As if this was the beginning of their final showdown. The young woman offered them a cruel smile. She was the only one who took pleasure from her sick and twisted games.

"Oh, maybe you haven't missed me, from the looks on your faces. But I guess, given that I had your boss killed and am controlling your old friend, there might be some bad blood between us. Such a shame that we can't all be friends, don't you think?"

"What do you want?" Brock snapped, his cheeks red with anger. Adeline held up her hands defensively, a look of feigned innocence on her pretty face.

"Whoa, so grouchy! I guess we can just cut to the chase, if that's what you want. You really do take the fun out of all this for me, though."

"Tell us why you're calling," Olivia said through gritted teeth. She, too, had no time for Adeline's cruel games. She was, after all, the Gamemaster—though she liked to be known as the Puppetmaster these days. But whenever they heard from her, it was far from a fun experience. She'd killed so many people in the name of entertainment. Whatever she had in mind, it would surely be a disaster for them and everyone they knew.

"Alright, I won't drag this out any longer. I suppose I'm here to invite you to the grand finale. A final showdown. I've been on the run for too long… and I'm ready for it to end. It's getting boring being better than everyone else. So here's the deal. One last round of fun. And if you do everything I say, if you play by the rules… you'll find me by the end. I might even hand myself over to you willingly."

"A likely story," Brock scoffed.

"Well, I suppose you'll find out, won't you?"

"You've already escaped from prison once. You've been lying to us for months. Why would we believe a word you say?" Brock countered. He'd been burned the worst by Adeline's challenges. It had nearly sent him over the edge more than once. Olivia understood his fury, though she knew giving into it only fed Adeline's joy at his suffering. She was still smiling, even as Brock trembled with anger.

"You don't have to believe me. But you do need to play. Because if you don't, you know there will be consequences," Adeline said darkly. Then she flashed them another grin. "But it doesn't have to come to that. I'm going to play fair, I swear it. Don't pull that face, Brock, it ruins your handsome face. I suppose you'll just have to wait and see if I keep my word. Here's my deal." She cleared her throat theatrically. "Roll up, roll up for the final challenge! Five is the magic number. I'm going to set up five challenges around the country over the next five weeks. You'll have exactly a week to complete each of the challenges, and the rules will change each time. Don't worry, though, these will be some of my best challenges yet. They will be complex, they will test your limits and blood *will be spilled...* if all goes to plan. Your challenge, should you choose to accept it, is to save a victim from certain death at the end of the week. There will be several clues, several hints, and several elements to find. They will be well hidden and you will need to find them. If you fail, people will die. If you succeed, you'll be heroes. You'll love that, won't you? That's what you guys seem to live for."

"It's our job to save people. We don't take pleasure in people dying, funnily enough. That's considered normal," Brock said, his eyes blazing. Adeline chuckled. She always knew how to push Brock's buttons in a way no one else could. She was his kryptonite, always finding new ways to torment him. While Olivia managed to keep a level head, it was more personal for him. She'd ensured that he lost so much.

"Well, there's nothing normal about me. I'm one of a kind. That's much more interesting than fitting into your little boxes. Even if I do have to do some crazy things to keep you on your toes. Come on, you've got to admit, life gets more interesting with me around. I think you'll miss me when I'm gone."

"Like a hole in the head," Brock muttered.

"Five challenges, five weeks, five locations...there's got to be more of a catch," Olivia said, brushing aside Adeline's goading comments. The sooner they got to the crux of what she was up to, the sooner they'd be able to get this whole mess out of the way. Adeline's eyes sparkled with mischief and she held up a finger.

"Ah, yes, the catch. Well, for starters, challenge number one will be to find a hostage without doing any police work. That means staying completely under cover and not being caught. It also means you can't tell your precious bosses where you're going or what you're doing. In fact, no one can find out what you're up to. I want to see if you fancy FBI agents are capable of much without all of your crutches."

"So we can't use *any* resources?" Olivia asked, frowning.

"I suppose you can find what you're looking for in the old-fashioned way. By getting on your hands and knees and fumbling around until you find something with your bare hands," Adeline smirked. "And did I mention that there will be obstacles? I'm sending an assassin on the exact same missions as you. He'll be trying to sabotage your efforts and find you before you can complete your tasks. If he finds you… he'll kill you. And believe me, he will. He's one of the best in the world. If he wants you dead, you're a goner."

Olivia sighed. If there was one thing Adeline Clarke knew how to do, it was how to exhaust her. She felt like she had been completely drained by the mess they'd landed themselves in. It had been a months-long game of cat and mouse. Adeline was the cat, playing with her food until the bitter end. But if this was truly the end of it all, then it would be worth it. They would finally be free of Adeline, and they could return to normality. If they could even figure out what that was anymore.

"If you break any of the rules, I'll have the hostage killed. And you know for sure you can trust me on that fact, don't you?" Adeline said with a cruel smile. "So I guess you'll want to get started, won't you? You have twenty-four hours to make it to St. Michael's—that's where your first hostage is. You'll need to work as a team to find the hostage, dead or alive. The clock will start counting down when your twenty-four hours is up. I may drop in to give you some clues along the way… but otherwise you're on your own. Don't tell anybody where you're going if you want the hostages to live. And definitely don't get the police or authorities involved. I mean it. The hostage will be dead the second you betray my trust."

Olivia almost snorted at the notion. They'd never trusted her for a second, and the idea that they could betray her was pretty rich given everything she'd done to them. But Olivia also knew better than to doubt Adeline's intentions. People always died when she was around, no matter how hard Olivia and Brock tried to stop it from happening. Either she gave them an impossible task or she broke her own rules to make sure someone got hurt. There was no winning for them when they played with the Gamemaster.

And Olivia had no doubt that this would be their most challenging task yet.

"Well, chop chop! Lots to do!" Adeline cheered, clapping her hands together brightly. It was still so unnerving. She should have been fluffing pom-poms for the football team with that kind of cheery enthusiasm. "And I know you've still got a burial to get to…don't worry, you'll still have plenty of time to get to St. Michael's. So sorry for your loss, Olivia. I hope the funeral gives you some closure for your cousin's death."

Olivia was about to roll her eyes, but Adeline's face was oddly sincere. Was this crazed, serial-killer-nightmare of a woman actually showing her some empathy? Olivia had no idea what to do if she was. But fortunately for her, Adeline's face broke into a grin once more.

"Let the games begin. Don't forget, St. Michael's, keep to yourselves and do not involve the police! Good luck. I'll be watching you."

CHAPTER TWO

Olivia and Brock arrived at St. Michael's in the middle of the night. They had left straight from Caro's funeral, not telling anyone where they were going or why. They couldn't risk anyone finding out about how they were being controlled, especially not Olivia's mother. Olivia knew that if they put even a single toe out of line, the Gamemaster would make everyone suffer for it, and that was a risk that Olivia wasn't willing to take, even for her own sake. People's lives were at stake, and that meant obeying the Gamemaster's every command. They drove in the dark, not speaking, holding their breaths as they quietly thought of the worst-case scenarios they might face once they arrived in St. Michael's.

The town itself was small and unassuming, a quiet fishing village with pretty stores and nice, unassuming houses that spoke to a comfortable existence. The air smelled of the sea and salt, and it looked like the kind of place where sunsets would be particularly beautiful to behold. At any other time, Olivia might have felt at home there, or maybe thought it was a nice place for a quick weekend vacation. But she wasn't there for a relaxing fishing weekend or to enjoy the town's history and museums, though they'd seen many signposts signaling them toward them. No, they had a life to save. And the fact they were on a timer—with only a week to complete their task—made the entire thing more stressful. Olivia didn't want to wait around and discover what would happen to their victim if they were unsuccessful.

And that was the problem—they didn't even have a clue of who they were looking for. A missing person, presumably, but given that they'd only just arrived and they still had a week to search, Olivia wasn't even sure the person in question would have been reported missing yet. It would be far too easy if they were, and Olivia was sure that the Gamemaster had snatched the person up mere minutes after ending her call to them to give them a weak start to the case. That would be just another cruel trick, a way to make their job even harder.

She had to wonder who the person might be and what they could've done to upset the Gamemaster enough to become tangled in one of her cruel games. The Gamemaster seemed like one for vengeance, one never to let any small slight go until the person has suffered much more than she ever had. But then again, sometimes, the way she chose people appeared to be random. Olivia and Brock had never even heard of her before she entangled them in her first game. She just liked to inflict pain and fear and was already succeeding. Olivia certainly felt afraid. Afraid of the price of failure.

But she knew by now how to push down her most terrifying thoughts or how to turn them into momentum on her cases. It was all a part of the job. And after the Gamemaster had made Yara kill Jonathan, Olivia had harbored a lifetime of fury, stored away for the perfect time when she could best wield it. Now, it was time to use that feeling to defeat the Gamemaster once and for all.

Brock parked the car outside the hotel they'd hastily booked on their way there, and silence took over them. It was like they'd both been winded by the knowledge that they were once again being swept up into a hellish case. Except this time, they were entirely on their own. They didn't have most of their tools and abilities at their disposal. They didn't have a team they could call for backup or other pairs of eyes to give insight into their task. No, they'd have to rely on themselves, their instincts, and their smarts. They were going to have to come up with some kind of inventive way to find their victim.

If only they knew *something* about the victim at hand.

Brock leaned his forehead against the steering wheel, looking defeated. It worried Olivia to see him when he'd had any kind of interaction with the Gamemaster. If anyone in the world knew how to get under his skin in the worst possible way, it was Adeline Clarke. She had put Brock through the wringer in particular, using his former friend as a puppet to inflict fear and pain, goading him whenever she slipped through their fingers again. Olivia saw what a toll it took on him to be involved in any case that included the Gamemaster. She worried about losing him to his anger again.

"How the hell are we going to do this?" he murmured, his voice sounding lost and desperate. She couldn't bear to see him that way. He was usually so strong. But she knew that everyone had a weakness. It didn't make him any lesser. If anything, it made her admire him more when he managed to push through it. Sometimes, he just needed support to make it through. Olivia touched his back, rubbing it gently.

"Hey. Don't give up before we've even started. It's looking rough, but we always come out on top. This time will be no different."

Brock sighed. "I know. But this feels different. I don't want to be negative, and yet I feel like this calls for some realism. This is some grand design by an absolute mastermind. Her only desire in life is to torture people, and she's set her sights on us. She's setting us up to fail because that's what she wants. She doesn't want us to succeed. And if she gets her way, five people will be dead within a month."

"Maybe. But she's also cocky. She underestimates what we're capable of. Haven't we made it through every test she's set for us so far? Where there's been a chance, we've taken it and made it through. She might've battered us a little along the way, but we persevered. She won't take us down this time."

Brock looked like he wanted to argue with Olivia, but he stopped himself at the last moment and smiled instead, reaching for her hand.

"You're right. There's no sense in giving up when we still don't know what we're dealing with. But this isn't going to be our typical case. If we can't ask questions or involve the police or the FBI...then we're going to have to think of something else. A new way to find out more about our victim."

"Well, right off the bat, we need to figure out a profile of who we're looking for. Right now, all we know is that there's someone being held hostage and that we need to find them. We don't even know if they're a man or a woman. And unless we can find missing person cases in the papers or online, our victim could literally be anyone from anywhere. They might not even be from this town..."

"It seems like an odd place to choose for this game, don't you think? I mean, it's a beautiful town, but there's not much going on here. Seems like if someone was missing here, it would be pretty obvious. You take someone out of a busy city, and they seem anonymous and easily forgotten. But here, you'd think they would be missed. Maybe not immediately, but someone would notice they're not around, right?"

"Assuming the person is from this town, then yes, perhaps you're right. But every town has its loners. There are some people that slip under the radar completely. Perhaps the Gamemaster would target someone like that. Someone who wouldn't be missed much, and someone that would be nearly impossible for us to find."

"But not completely, hopefully," Brock said with a deep sigh. "So how are we supposed to gather information? We need to be able to speak to people and get a sense of them while we are in the town. We can't just stop people on the street to talk to them; we can't just waltz into the police station and try to glean information without causing suspicion. If we do, people will ask us questions we're not allowed to answer and things will get messy fast. We're going to need a different approach."

Olivia chewed her lip. "Ideally, we need an efficient way of collecting data that doesn't make us look like cops. Some way to get people talking that doesn't seem like it's coming from a place of nosiness. If someone figures out who we are, then our victim will die. There's no doubt about that."

"Then we're going to need to be extra careful. Any ideas?"

Olivia considered the question for a few moments. What would give them access to numerous people and get them chatting to people? And what would also give them a reason to be at people's houses, looking for clues of something amiss? She could only think of one way to do something so invasive, and it was a risk. She sighed, glancing at Brock.

"I might have an idea. You're not going to like it, though."

Brock raised his eyebrows. "What is it?"

"We could pretend to be door-to-door salesmen. It gives us an excuse to be ringing people's doorbells. We can take note of houses with no responses maybe get a read on the places and people we visit. We can check for suspicious characters and, get close to the houses, look through the windows to see if there are any signs of disturbances. But obviously, it means playing a role, and it's not perfect..."

"It sounds like a nightmare."

"I know. But if you haven't got any other ideas..."

"I've got an idea. We do *anything* but that."

Olivia rolled her eyes. "I'm open to suggestions. But I do think there's a lot we can get out of this method. I don't see how else we're going to get up close and personal with the locals. It might be the only way."

"But there are hundreds of houses and we don't have time on our side. We might get lucky, but we also might just waste hours and hours to get nowhere. It might tell us nothing."

"I know. But I don't know what else we can do to find excuses to be speaking to people. Maybe we can visit the town hall and see if there's any information there about the locals, or a town meeting might enlighten us to some information. But we still need a way to be undercover. And the one guarantee we have is that people will open their doors if the bell rings."

"You call that a guarantee? We deliberately never answer our doorbell unless we're expecting guests... or a pizza delivery..."

"Okay, maybe it's not a sure thing. But it's something." Olivia rubbed at her temples. She could feel a headache forming behind her eyes—always a telltale sign of stress getting the better of her. She couldn't afford that right now. She knew she needed to rest if she was going to be alert enough to investigate.

"It's late. Maybe we can sleep on it and come up with something better in the morning. But we can't afford to wait around until a better idea comes to us. Unless you can come up with something by the morning, we're going with my plan. Okay?"

Brock's mouth turned up in a flirtatious smile. "So authoritative. I like it."

Olivia rolled her eyes again, but she managed to smile. Even in their darkest times, Brock always knew how to raise a smile out of her. But it didn't take long for her anxiety to take hold of her once again. It had been a long time since she'd felt so unsure about a case. They were fish out of water with no sense of how to get back to the sea. For the first time, they were working with absolutely nothing. No clues, no tools, and no intuition. How could they even begin to guess what they were searching for when they were in a town they'd never visited, surrounded by strangers who meant nothing to them?

They got out of the car and checked into the hotel with a grumpy receptionist before heading to their room. They hadn't even had much time to pack, and Olivia didn't see much point in taking anything out of her hastily stuffed bag. She had no idea where the next mini-case would take them, but she was sure they'd be up and moving again within the week. Assuming they managed to solve the case on time, that was. She just hoped that her plan might work, slapdash as it felt to both her and Brock. She was starting to hope some epiphany might come to her in a dream.

"Olivia…"

"Hmm?" Olivia said, breaking out of her thoughts. Brock held up his phone to her, showing that he had a new message.

"I think we have our first clue."

Olivia rushed to Brock's side, eager for anything the Gamemaster might've sent to them. He opened the message to see that a voice note had been sent in the chat. Olivia's heart somersaulted. Whatever was on the voice note was likely going to be spine-chilling, but there was no time to waste. Olivia reached for the phone and pressed play on the voice note.

The sound of heavy breathing filled their ears. It sounded like a woman, and she seemed to be terrified. She let out a strangled sob.

"Please, please, you've got to find me," she screeched. "I'm all alone, and I'm terrified. She's going to kill me. Please, you have to—"

The voice note cut off there. Olivia swallowed, glancing at Brock. She could feel a chill creeping up her spine. The woman's fear was embedded into her very bones.

"So we're looking for a woman, then," Olivia said. Brock nodded, still a little shaken by the voice note.

"Most likely. But we can't always trust the Gamemaster. This could be a red herring. She does love to misdirect us. It wouldn't be out of the realm of possibility for her to have another victim on standby to get that voice note from. Or an actress doing her bidding."

Olivia chewed her lip, her stomach twisting... "You don't think... you don't think that was Yara, do you?"

Brock shook his head immediately.

"No. I'd know her voice anywhere. And she's not that good of an actress to change her voice that much. No, the Gamemaster won't kill her. At least not yet."

The dark comment made Olivia feel cold. Had it really come to this?

Brock seemed to be thinking along the same lines. He rolled his shoulders back, straightening up with a determined look on his face.

"I think we should keep our options open, looking for any signs of a missing person. And failing a better plan, we'll start going door to door in the morning." He sighed. "I guess we're going to have to figure out what it is that we're selling..."

CHAPTER THREE

OLIVIA AND BROCK WOKE UP EARLY ON THE FIRST DAY of their investigation. No alarms were necessary—Olivia felt as though the sheer pressure of the week ahead of them crushed her lungs and jolted her to life before even the sun was up. Olivia headed to the hotel lobby to grab a local newspaper as they ordered room service to prepare them for the day. She took it back to bed with her, sipping coffee as she skipped through it, looking for anything of interest.

"I don't think there's anyone reported missing yet," Olivia said to Brock as he plowed through a bacon sandwich. "I mean, in a small town like this, I imagine that would be pretty big news, right? Someone just disappearing into thin air."

"Depends how much they matter to the community, I suppose. Not everyone is always bothered about a missing person. It's a sad fact, but a true one," Brock said, wiping sauce from the corner of his mouth. "The Gamemaster must have had this plan in motion for a long time. Or at least there was some kind of forward planning. She had plenty of time to pick a victim, to watch out for someone who would slip beneath the radar. We know one thing for certain—she's more than happy to see us fail. And if that means finding the perfect victim... someone that no one cares about... then she'll do it, surely?"

Olivia nodded. They'd faced so many challenges before, but this was something else. The timer they'd been put on made an impossible task even harder. How were they supposed to search for someone when they had no idea who they were looking for? It was like trying to find an invisible needle in a haystack. They were feeling around blindly, hoping to stumble across something that might help them.

"Maybe we'll have more luck online," Brock suggested, pulling out his phone. "Newspapers are kind of old-school these days. The internet will give us more immediacy. Especially given that we're looking at yesterday's paper. But maybe it's still too early to tell."

As suspected, Brock's search came up with little of interest. It was just too soon. It wasn't often they began investigating a case before a body showed up, or at least before they had a clue to work with. Maybe the police had information that they didn't, but they also didn't have any clue about the pressure of the clock and didn't know who they were dealing with. Plus, they weren't able to ask them any questions the way they would've before. The circumstances were unusual, and it wasn't about to make their lives any easier. But Olivia prepared as best as she could for the day. They agreed that until they had more to work with, their door-to-door tactic was going to have to do.

"So, what's the product we're selling?" Olivia asked. "It's going to have to be decent if we want to keep people at the door..."

"What if we just say we're asking for signatures for some sort of petition? Maybe get people involved in the community?"

Olivia chuckled. "That's the easiest way to get the door slammed in your face."

"Maybe we should say we're working for a charity. A little guilt tripping goes a long way..."

"It also might make people willing to give us money, and then we're going to get done for fraud."

"That would be a fun twist in the plot..."

"We want something that's going to keep people at the door for at least a minute or so, but that seems like something they don't actually want to buy... I guess cleaning products is always a safe bet, right? Maybe some bleach or something... we can grab a bottle on our way out and at least have a prop to work with."

"I've got to admit, I hate this plan even more than when you came up with it."

"Me too, believe me. The last thing I want to do is harass people in their homes while also being nosy. But I'm hoping we'll get at least some information out of it. I think you should do the selling, though."

Brock wrinkled his nose. "Why me?"

"Because you're the charming one. Charisma evades me when I need it most. You're a walking flirt, and you'll keep people talking for longer."

Brock smirked, messing with the collar of his shirt with a flirty glint in his eye. "What a way to stroke my ego."

"I think your ego is always pretty well stroked. But whatever works. You'll do it?"

"Fine. But if I'm too good at my job and we end up selling out of bleach, then don't blame me. The people of St. Michael's aren't going to know what hit them. Watch out, ladies and gentlemen, Storm Brock is coming your way."

Olivia gave him a tired smile. She was usually on board with Brock's cheekiness, but their case was so troublesome that she felt like she needed to put her all into it, and that meant there was no time for messing around. They couldn't afford to let this investigation slip through their fingers. They couldn't even be sure that the clue the Gamemaster had given them was trustworthy, and that put them at square one. They would need to handle this as though they were walking blindly in the dark. It was terrifying, to put it simply. But Olivia knew that focusing on her fear wouldn't help. She had to tap into her logic, into the side of herself that ran off instinct and skill. And she knew that even in the most desperate times, those things had never failed her.

It was around eight when they headed out into the town. Olivia thought it was probably too early for their plans, but she didn't want to waste a moment, and she couldn't see how else to spend their time. They drove to the furthest edge of the town, where handsome houses lined up in well-spaced rows, gardens pruned to perfection. It was a nice neighborhood, the kind Olivia could imagine seeing in a montage at the beginning of a movie about a small town with a dark secret. And she guessed that was exactly what St. Michael's was at the moment. But they were the only ones in on the secret. And that was an enormous weight to carry on their shoulders.

The neighborhood was coming alive for the day. People were starting to leave their houses for work, to take their children to school, to run errands, and seize the day. Olivia clutched her notepad in her hands, marking down the name of the street. She planned to note down anything she thought might be of interest to them. Houses where no one answered the door. Houses where something inside seemed to be amiss. Houses where someone was acting suspiciously at the door. It wasn't much to go off, and she knew that the majority of the information she gleaned would turn out to mean nothing. But for now, they had no better way to canvass the area and get a feel for the people of the town. They just had to hope that something interesting would come out of their efforts while also keeping one eye on the local news.

"Let's get this over and done with," Brock said, some of his bravado from earlier being replaced by miserable resignation. Apparently, his confidence didn't stretch to door-to-door sales.

Olivia began scribbling notes as they walked down the street once, noting houses where ordinary activity seemed to be going on. They agreed that they'd walk the street once, making notes this way, and then they'd start knocking on doors. But nothing seemed amiss in the neighborhood. There were no sketchy people milling around. No one looked twice at the two strangers walking down their road. No one was on edge or fearful of what they might face that day. As a collective, they seemed completely at ease. And why wouldn't they? Most likely, none of them had a clue that somewhere in their small town, a person was being held against their will, seven days away from being killed for perhaps no reason. They had no idea that they shouldn't feel safe a single day of their lives, that there were madmen and assassins running around their hometown. They didn't live on the edge the way Olivia had for so long.

As they reached the end of the road, her frantic scribbles on her page looked like something written by a crazed person. When had they fallen so far down the rabbit hole? When had their reality warped into one long, sick game of hide and seek? She cursed the Gamemaster beneath her breath. She prayed that they could find answers and strike the Gamemaster where it hurt. But she was also wary of the fact that this might possibly be the first time where victory simply wasn't possible. She'd have to steel herself for that possibility.

"Alright. Where do we start?" Brock asked. Olivia checked her notes.

"I guess we start at number one. We didn't see any signs of life from them yet."

"Right. We start from the beginning," Brock said with a sigh. He rolled his shoulders back, looking uncomfortable in his collared shirt, a bottle of supermarket bleach clutched in his hands. Their efforts were a little pitiful, but they no longer had the luxury of time or options. Brock cleared his throat.

"Okay. I've got this."

They strode up the driveway of number one. Inside, Olivia could hear morning cacophony. It sounded like kids were playing somewhere inside, and a mother's voice was raising to try and regain some control. Olivia and Brock exchanged a look.

"This seems like an unlikely candidate for trouble," Olivia said. "Maybe let's start at number two."

"Fine by me."

They moved on to the next house. Unlike number one, there were no signs of life inside the house. This time, Brock didn't hesitate before knocking on the door. Now that the sun was starting to rise, Olivia was sure that most of the neighborhood would be awake. Brock's loud rapping on the door couldn't be ignored. Slowly, Olivia heard signs of movement inside, and an old man came to the door, shrouded in a striped dressing gown. He scowled at them, looking Brock up and down.

"What do you want?"

Brock fixed the man his biggest smile. "Good morning, sir! How are you this morning?"

"I'm not happy. I've got two idiots on my doorstep grinning at me when they don't even know me. What are you doing here?"

While Brock tried his marketing pitch on the man, Olivia looked for signs of anything amiss inside, but saw little out of place. That wasn't unexpected, especially when she still didn't really know what she was looking for. Upturned furniture, perhaps, or a sign of a struggle. But it was just the old man and his attitude residing in this house.

"I don't want any damn bleach," the man said, slamming the door in their faces. Brock blinked several times in shock. Clearly he hadn't been expecting such a frustrated response.

"So much for my charm. I guess it doesn't work on grumpy old guys," Brock said with a sniff. Olivia couldn't help smiling, hiding it behind her hand. Finally, Brock had found a place where even his charm wasn't enough to save him from the wrath of others.

Their mission was impossibly slow progress, though, and soon, Olivia and Brock were both fed up. Olivia made notes as they walked, noting missing cars, closed curtains and no-shows, but the information wasn't giving them much other than endless sheets of notes that they couldn't do much with. None of the information they'd gathered was indicative of a missing person, and there was no way to tell what their data was useful for. They were used to reading between the lines, thinking outside of the box, and looking for things that others might have missed, but there was a complete absence of sense to the information they were collecting. By the time they'd visited one block of houses, the sun was well and truly up, and they had little to show for their efforts. As they wearily went up an empty driveway, Olivia took a desperate peek in through the window.

"This is pointless," she said grouchily. "How are we supposed to know what we're looking for? There's no car here, but they could've just gone out for the day. Or slept in. Or maybe they're ignoring us..."

"Hey! What are you doing, snooping in people's windows? Go away!" a neighbor snapped from across the street as she was getting into her car. She was so stern that Olivia and Brock immediately began to leave, not wanting to cause any trouble. The Gamemaster had been very clear with them—don't draw attention and get into trouble. They wordlessly returned to their car, Brock miserably clutching his bleach with exhaustion crossing his face.

"Well, what now?" he asked. Olivia sighed.

"I think we need a new plan."

CHAPTER FOUR

"**W**ELL, THAT WAS UNPRODUCTIVE," BROCK SAID AS they got back in the car. "And we've barely covered a tenth of the town. We haven't learned anything at all."

"We don't know that yet," Olivia said. "You never know when some small detail will come back and help you out. But I'll admit, I don't think we can continue this way. It's certainly not sustainable. And now that we've drawn attention to ourselves a little too much, I think we need to be careful about how we decide to go forward. The last thing we want is to misstep and get our victim killed ahead of time."

"That's if this assassin hasn't gotten there before us," Brock said miserably. "It's insane. The things the Gamemaster puts us through… it's inhuman."

"I know. But getting angry at our situation isn't going to help matters at all. And you know what? I think we've been missing something obvious from the start."

Brock raised an eyebrow. "You do?"

"Yes. We've been scrabbling around to find out more details about our victim… Normally that kind of information is handed to us the moment we find a dead body, or when we're given a profile of someone who has gone missing. But we have to flip this on its head. Normally, we're trying to build a profile for a faceless killer long before we know who they are or what they want. But we know the Gamemaster. At least, we know some things. And I think we need to use that to our advantage right now. We need to note down what we know and try to figure out the kind of person the Gamemaster is likely to target based on that."

Brock thumped his forehead with his palm. "How did we not think of that right away?"

"We've been under a lot of pressure, focusing on all of the things we *can't* do. The Gamemaster told us not to use any of our usual methods because she thinks we'll alert the police. But we're still federal agents. We have tools at our disposal without getting anyone else involved. We *can* do this. We'll just need to be a bit more calculated about our efforts."

"Well, this beats going door to door, at least. Let's find somewhere to get a coffee and something to eat while we ponder this one. And we can finally put that notepad to better use…"

Fifteen minutes later, they were residing in a small cafe in the town center. Olivia felt very much in need of the coffee that arrived at their table while she was starting a new page of the notepad, raring to go once again. She kept her voice low as she smoothed the paper down and clicked her pen.

"Alright, so what do we know about the Gamemaster for sure?"

"She's a pain in the butt."

"A given. What else?"

Brock chewed his lip. "She likes to toy with people. And she's a compulsive liar. She gets a thrill from misdirecting us, which is why any of her clues can't really be trusted. But she never lies about things that she's serious about. Like what she'll do to us or the victims when we step out of line."

Olivia nodded in agreement. In her mind, she was back on the island, watching bodies drop to the ground for breaking the rules. They could always trust the Gamemaster to stick to her word when it came to killing people.

"Okay, what else? What about the people she targets?"

"Hmm, that's a tricky one. When she arranged for the jet to go down on the island, she knew she was targeting the rich and privileged. I think she took some joy from being able to mess with the untouchable, if that makes any sense. She liked the idea that even though the rich and famous can usually come away unscathed from anything, she had some kind of power over them. But I don't think she hates the elite. She came from a very rich family herself. Unless there's some kind of internalized hate there for the world she grew up in … but then again, she couldn't do any of this kind of thing if she didn't have money in her pocket. So it seems a little hypocritical if those are her targets."

Olivia nodded. "I don't think she's overly concerned with seeming like a hypocrite. In fact, I don't think she cares much what anyone thinks. She craves fame and attention, positive or negative. She's not particular about it. She just wants to be seen and heard whenever she decides to crawl out of the woodwork. I mean, she's been biding her time, coming up with this five-week torture scheme for the pair of us. Why? Because it makes her relevant again. She knew she had to come back with a flair after the last time … and she also knows that she's a threat that we'll take seriously. I think she likes that. And of course, she likes to make things personal. She's kept Yara on board this entire time, making her the centerpiece of each of her games. Because she knows it bothers us. And then Jonathan? He'd never done anything to her in particular, but she roped him in to fight us on the boat, and she had him killed without blinking an eye…"

"Because she knew it would mean something to us. Her favorite playthings. But also… I think she took pleasure in taking down such a high-ranking member of the FBI. To her, that's the cherry on top, because he had power and influence. So maybe she doesn't care about taking down the rich… but she has a problem with authority figures. Because they're the ones trying to always control her."

Olivia took a deep breath and began to scribble down some notes. Now, they were finally getting somewhere. The importance of building a profile of the Gamemaster had slipped her mind before, but now she knew that this was going to be useful to helping them figure out who their victims might be. Complex as the Gamemaster was, she was a puzzle to be solved by herself. And even the most challenging puzzles fit together in the end, given time and effort to figure them out. The Gamemaster, like anyone, had strengths, weaknesses, and holes in her armor that they could use to their advantage. Now she felt sure that this was how they would take her down and make sure she didn't win again.

"So we know a little more now about who she tends to target… but do we think there's any soft spots she has?" Olivia asked. "I have a feeling that she's softer on mothers. You remember how she made space in her games so that Rose could be let go? A pregnant woman… she had mercy. She hadn't realized she would be on the plane that day, and she hadn't wanted her to die. So either she has respect for mothers or for children. Maybe both."

"I suppose so. What do we know about her own mother? It sounds like she spent a lot of time away at work, focusing on money and building an empire. Wouldn't be surprised if she neglected her daughter a little, right?"

Olivia couldn't help but smile skeptically. "You think she's doing all this out of mommy issues?"

Brock shrugged. "Hey, I've seen firsthand how those can manifest…"

"For your sake, I'm going to ignore that…"

"But seriously. Maybe she harbors some sort of desire to always impress the woman who birthed her, wanting to be loved and noticed. Perhaps she was given just enough to keep admiring her and caring about her. If she idolized her mother, it would make sense that she has respect for women who raise children."

"None of the women on the island had children, aside from Rose being pregnant. It's only a small correlation, but it seems like it could be kind of a big deal where Adeline is concerned. And if the person we're looking for is in fact, a woman, as the voice note suggested, then perhaps we need to be looking for someone who doesn't have children. It would also help to support the theory that the Gamemaster is likely targeting a victim that won't be obviously missing right away to make our job harder. So, not someone with children. Likely someone who lives alone. Unmarried or divorced, maybe. Someone who isn't active in the community, someone who doesn't show their face around enough to be obviously missing right off the bat. Maybe even someone who doesn't permanently live here, who commutes out of town for work a lot, or generally doesn't hang around." Olivia continued to scribble notes down on her pad of paper, sipping coffee with her free hand. "Perhaps we have more to work with than we originally thought."

"There's a lot to consider. Who would the Gamemaster actively have an issue with? Going back to authority figures… what about politicians? Police officers?"

"Maybe, but we'd know by now if a political figure or police officer went missing. That's front page newsworthy."

"True. Okay, maybe it's time to consider how we might search for someone that fits the profile for the victim. How are we supposed to find a woman who flies under the radar completely?"

Brock scratched at his chin. "I don't know. I mean, this isn't a huge town, but it's significantly big enough that we're still going to be grasping at straws with what little information we have. A lot of what we've come up with is speculation, too. But small towns love gossip. Loners in a close-knit community tend to stand out and get talked about. Maybe this is a chance for you to go undercover."

"How so?"

"Get involved in community activities, claim you're new to the area, and try to make sense of the gossip mill. Eventually someone might talk and we might glean something about a missing person. The thing is, someone who is disliked in a community comes up in conversation even more than you'd expect. The second they do or don't do something they're supposed to, it's suddenly everyone's business. What if we can find something else that way?"

"And what would you do while I'm swanning around gossiping with the locals?"

"I could keep going door to door, I guess. I can dig in other ways. Keep an eye on the news. It could be worth a try."

Olivia chewed her lip. "I don't know if I've got enough time to insert myself into the community this way... people are going to need to trust me to be able to talk about these things with me. And that's going to take time."

"Maybe. But a fresh face is always welcome in a small town. You'll be like meat in a pack of lions. They won't be able to resist jumping on you."

"But doesn't this draw attention our way?"

"In a way, but no one is going to know who you are or what you're looking for. You're not going to seem suspicious to a group of people who don't realize what's at stake. We can spend the afternoon building a character for you to play, and then once we've made you into a believable person, we can insert you into a few places, play your hand, and see how it goes. It's still the first day... but if a plan like this is going to need room to work, we have to start now. Is it worth a try, do you think?"

Olivia nodded. "You're probably right." A smile played on her lips. "The salesman and the gossip queen... what a pair we make. Let's talk about building me a story."

CHAPTER
FIVE

OLIVIA WAS NO LONGER OLIVIA KNIGHT. SHE WAS ANGIE Broadhurst, a young woman who had just broken up with her boyfriend and was looking for a new start in a new town. She loved to try out new hobbies and get involved in local politics, and she loved a strong community vibe.

It was exactly the opposite of Olivia on a normal day. She preferred to mind her own business and keep to herself. But she knew that she'd really have to sell the role if she was going to get people talking to her in the town. And she had to be convincing because if anyone found out who she really was and why she was in town, then she would blow the entire task, and someone would end up dead.

Olivia hoped going undercover would allow her to chat with some of the other people in the community and maybe find out if anything was amiss. On their second day in St. Michael's, she donned her friendliest smile and headed out alone, leaving Brock to the task of continuing going door to door. She couldn't help thinking that he would be better suited to the task—people tended to warm to Brock very quickly, especially women. His handsome face and endless charisma were some of his greatest weapons. But it was too late to change the plan, and Olivia knew she was up to the task as well. It just might not come as naturally to her.

Her first stop was the local flower arranging class. She had spent the entire previous evening signing up for all sorts of classes at the community center—flower arranging would take up an hour of her morning, followed immediately by cake decorating. After lunch, there was a coffee hour set up in the main hall, and in the evening, there was a wine tasting. Olivia hoped that each class would be a great place to get involved in the gossip mill, to get talking to people and finding out more about the town's inner workings.

But as the day went on, she began to lose hope. The flower arranging class was full of semi-professionals who had no interest in chatting, so Olivia left with thorns in her fingers and little to work with. The cake decorating class wasn't much better, and Olivia struggled to keep up with the instructions as she sloppily arranged icing on her cake, her fingers still sore from flower arranging. She was beginning to worry that she had wasted an entire morning of their investigation time with learning skills that she'd never use again.

But when the coffee hour began and Olivia sidled into the main hall, she hoped for a miracle. She surveyed the room, looking for somewhere she could slip in and get chatting to someone. She felt like she was back at high school, not knowing where she would fit in or whether anyone would be interested in talking to her.

But that was when she felt someone's arm link through hers. She turned and saw a woman not much older than her smiling at her. She recognized her from both of the classes she'd attended that morning, and she seemed to be some kind of expert in both. She wore pink lipstick and soft eyeshadow, her bleached hair cut into a perfectly straight bob. She looked exactly like the kind of woman who had secrets resting on her tongue just waiting to be whispered in her ear.

"Hi there," the woman said with a smile. "You're new around here, aren't you? I haven't seen you here before."

"Yes! I am!" Olivia said, glad that someone had come to her instead of having to find a place to slot herself in. "I'm Angie. I just moved to town."

"Nice to meet you, Angie! I'm Mira. Everyone around here knows me as the local housewife... except I don't have a husband or kids, and I don't do any chores!"

Olivia let out a pleasant laugh, though she wasn't sure whether Mira was joking or not. "Well what a life that sounds like!"

"Oh, it suits me just fine. The perks of a hefty inheritance," Mira laughed in return. "Two classes in one day, hmm? Are you trying to find a new hobby?"

"Yeah... I guess I'm just looking for a completely fresh start here. I just split from my boyfriend..."

Mira gripped Olivia's arm hard. "Say no more. You're looking to reinvent yourself to start anew! Well, I can help with that. It's official. I'm taking you under my wing! Come and sit with me and the girls. We'll let you know *exactly* what's what in this town."

Olivia smiled, feeling triumphant. If Mira knew anything of worth, then she was about to hand it all to Olivia on a silver platter.

Olivia was introduced to a group of four other ladies at one of the tables and she sat down with them, making polite chatter about why she'd moved to town and what she hoped to get out of the place. She hoped the focus would soon move away from her, and it did after around twenty minutes of grilling. Olivia tuned in as the women began to gossip about the things that had happened since their last coffee morning the previous week.

"Did you hear that Sasha is pregnant *again?*"

"I can't believe that Bella's husband got demoted after they just bought that new car..."

"Doesn't Rosa's garden look an absolute mess this year?"

"I heard that Gayle was caught kissing Brad during a very intimate dinner this week..."

Olivia patiently listened to the endless chatter, hoping to mine some gold out of the conversation. But as the afternoon went on, she began to feel as though they weren't really getting anywhere. It wasn't until Mira piped up that Olivia finally felt a slither of hope.

"Hey, ladies. Did you hear that Flora moved out?"

"That weird woman who lives on the edge of town?" one of the other women scoffed. "Good riddance. She didn't fit in here *at all.*"

"That's old news," another of the women dismissed. "She's been gone for days."

"But does anyone know *why* she left?" Mira asked with a conspiratorial smile. Olivia's ears perked up, and she sat up a little straighter.

"What happened?" she asked. Mira smirked.

"Well, nobody knows. That's the thing, it was all very sudden."

"I think she just couldn't stand to be here any longer when she knows no one likes her," one of the ladies dismissed. "It's no big deal."

"But the house only went up for sale last week. It's still on sale... but she's gone. Rumor has it that a car came to her house in the middle of the night... and the next morning, when her neighbor went over to check on her, she was gone. All of her furniture was gone, too. She's not been back since."

Olivia's heart began to pound. She knew there were a thousand explanations for what might have happened to Flora. She could've gone away on a vacation, but that didn't explain the missing furniture. Perhaps she'd just found somewhere else to live while she waited for the house to sell.

But the curious part of her felt differently. What was with the mysterious car in the middle of the night? And why was all of her furniture suddenly gone? It was the kind of disappearing act that had the Gamemaster written all over it. And Flora fit the kind of profile they were looking for—a woman who didn't fit into the community, someone who would only be missed by the local women desperate for someone to gossip about.

Olivia knew she would have to follow up on the lead. It was the only thing she had so far, and though it was a loose lead, it was something. She was already formulating a plan, trying to figure out how she could prove that Flora was missing without rousing suspicion or using any police work. She'd need a reason to try and contact her, or a means to.

"Say... there's a house for sale?" Olivia asked the women. "I'm renting at the moment, but I'm looking for something more permanent."

"Oh my goodness, I would just *love* it if you bought her house. You're so much fun!" Mira declared. "Here... I'll find the listing for you. You can call the realtor and get a quote. I'm sure that Flora will be so desperate to get rid of the house that she'll cut you a deal."

Olivia took the information gratefully. As the coffee hour drew to a close, she couldn't get out of there fast enough—though she promised to see Mira later that evening for the wine tasting workshop.

Olivia found the number for the realtor and gave them a call.

"Hi... My name is Angie Broadhurst, I'm looking to buy in the area. I would just *love* to speak to the owner of the house on the edge of town... Flora, is it? I was given this number by a friend of hers who said she would be interested in talking about selling up."

Olivia negotiated for a while on the phone before she was able to get a hold of Flora's phone number, but after half an hour of answering questions, they finally allowed her to have it. Then, with shaking hands, Olivia dialed the number, praying that Flora wouldn't pick up. If she didn't, then it was possible she was the missing woman she was searching for.

One ring.

Two rings.

Three rings.

There was no answer.

Olivia held her breath. Was this the woman whose voice she had heard on the voice note? Was her disappearance in the middle of the night really the work of the Gamemaster? Were they the first people to notice she was gone?

Olivia was shocked when her phone began to ring in her hand. It was the number she had just called. Was the Gamemaster about to speak to her on the other end of the line? Or she could allow Flora to give her some sort of a clue. Olivia prayed that this was what she had been waiting for. She picked up the phone, waiting for something to happen…

"Hi! I'm so sorry to have missed your call… I never answer an unknown number, but my realtor just texted to say that you might try to get in contact! Are you interested in the house?"

Olivia let out a sigh. It had been a shot in the dark, but it was a disappointing letdown all the same.

Perhaps the gossip mill wasn't so useful after all.

CHAPTER SIX

Despite Olivia's best efforts in her undercover mission, not much came of her time spent among the women of the community. She heard plenty of gossip but none that pointed in the direction of a missing person. And as the days continued on, she grew more anxious. She barely slept at night, lying awake for torturous long hours trying to think of solutions to their mystery. Not to mention, she didn't feel safe, knowing there was apparently an assassin hunting them down. But as the week started to close, they were no closer to answers than they had been before.

And Brock didn't have any answers either. He'd been scouring the town for clues, reading up on the local news, and hoping for a miracle, but they still had no indication of their missing person. It was as though someone had completely disappeared from the town, and it had completely escaped everyone's notice.

"I think we need to go to the police station," Olivia said eventually on the fifth night of their investigations. They were sitting in their hotel room, picking at their room service meal. Brock looked at her as though she had gone crazy.

"That's the one thing we were told not to do. If we involve the police in our investigation, the Gamemaster will kill the victim right off the bat."

"I know we're not allowed to speak with the police... but we're not getting any closer to answers... and we weren't told that we can't listen in at the police station. I'm not suggesting we speak to anyone. I think we could go undercover and see if we hear anything of interest. Maybe I could go in and file a fake report to give me a reason to hang around and listen in. Surely that doesn't break any of the rules?"

Brock chewed his lip. "I don't know... it's risky. Do we really want to chance it? This is someone's life we are potentially playing with."

"And we only have two days left before the Gamemaster kills them. If we don't find out something soon, they're dead anyway. I know it's a risk, and I don't like the idea of playing risky games any more than you do. But we're being set up to fail, and you know it. We're no closer to the truth than we were five days ago. I hate to say it... but I don't think we can solve this without a boost. You know I don't like to be defeatist, but we have to be real about this. What's better—to take a risk that might pay off... or to leave the victim's fate in the hands of the Gamemaster in two days' time?"

Brock's face was creased with worry, and Olivia understood entirely. She was asking him to take a person's life into their hands more than ever before. It was a hard decision to make. If the Gamemaster killed someone for them bending the rules, they would forever have that on their conscience. But Olivia didn't want anyone to die, and she felt sure that if they carried on the way they were going that someone would be dead by the end of the week. It was a certainty versus a chance. She didn't like taking risks at the best of times, but when she had a good reason to, she was willing to try.

"Okay. If you think this is the best course of action, then you know I trust you. I'll always follow your lead," Brock said. Olivia reached out and squeezed his hand.

"Thank you. I think this might be our last chance… it's got to be worth a try. I'll need a backstory, though. A reason to go into the station and stick around a while. If I file a report, it's got to be something where the police aren't going to try and take me to be questioned immediately. Something where they're just willing to let me sit down and fill out a report rather than taking me too seriously."

Brock thought for a moment. "Maybe something where they don't need too much information… a speeding violation, maybe? You can say that you saw someone speeding and driving dangerously, and you wanted to report the license plate. They're not going to ask too many questions about that. You can probably stall with a form for a while in there."

"Then let's get this moving. We don't have time to waste."

The police station was busy when Olivia arrived, which she took to be a good thing. The fact that it was busy meant she could blend into the background. Or so she hoped. She didn't want to have anyone asking her too many questions. She was already taking a risk by setting foot in a police station, but she had to hope that she wasn't breaking the rules simply by being there. An officer caught her eye as she approached the front desk. She wondered if the Gamemaster somehow had a plant there at the station, keeping an eye on things and making sure Olivia and Brock toed the line. She wouldn't put it past her.

But she'd made it this far, so she supposed that turning back wouldn't do her any good now. She approached the reception after waiting in line and met with a grouchy-looking man behind the desk.

"Hi. I'd like to report an incident of speeding and dangerous driving."

The man sighed. "Really? It's a very busy day here…can't you just let the speed cameras do their job?"

"What speed cameras? I don't think I've seen a single one in this town. It's not safe!" Olivia said indignantly. It wasn't a lie—the town seemed to have very little in place to prevent speeding violations. The man sighed and picked up a form and a clipboard. He shoved them in Olivia's direction, clearly trying not to roll his eyes.

"Fill out this form and bring it back to me. You'll need the license plate for the car that was speeding. The form explains itself."

"Thank you," Olivia said, taking the form. The guy might be grouchy and frustrating, but he'd just secured her undercover mission. She moved through the crowds of people to sit in the waiting area, propping the clipboard on her knee and clicking her pen. But she didn't start writing. There weren't any eyes on her, and she was tucked away enough that she knew no one would be paying attention to what she was doing. She kept her eyes trained on the page in front of her, but her ears were listening out for anything of interest. She wasn't sure how long she'd get away with sitting there, but she was willing to wait all day if it got her anywhere with the case. She hoped that by the time she walked out of there, she would have the name of someone who had been reported missing or at least some kind of lead to someone who might be their victim.

Hours passed by slowly. Occasionally, Olivia would lift her pen and write something on the sheet of paper just to avoid suspicion, but no one really looked her way. The place was bustling, which surprised Olivia for such a small town. There was someone who came in for being drunk and disorderly, and Olivia witnessed a very heated argument between two local youths who had been arrested for fighting on the streets. But there was nothing about a missing person. Olivia began to wonder if she was wasting her time. Brock had been spending his day trying to do more research, looking for clues, and all she'd done was sit, listening out, and twiddling a pen in her fingers. She started to doubt her plan and wondered whether she should just leave and try to assist Brock. But something made her stay. She tended to trust her gut, and it was telling her to stick around for a little longer. So she sat tight, anxiety knotted in her stomach as her presence in the police station began to seem more and more unnatural. She could tell that some of the others in the waiting area were starting to clock her and see that she really meant to be there. She found herself actually filling out the form for something to do, to validate her presence there.

But it wasn't much longer before Olivia hit the jackpot. She could hear a woman's voice cutting through the crowds and Olivia glanced up momentarily to see a plump woman with curly hair following a police officer through the station, a look of desperation on her face.

"You're not listening to me. My boyfriend is missing. He hasn't replied to me in days. That's not normal for him."

"Ma'am, we're very busy around here. I'm sorry your boyfriend didn't reply to his messages, but I don't know what you want us to do about that."

"No, you don't understand…you need to give me a chance to explain myself. I should have reported this sooner. It's not like him to not message me. I've been out of town, so I guess I just thought he was busy and couldn't reply to me. But it's been six days since his last message, and I was worried. So I went over to his place to see if there was something going on…I don't know, maybe I thought he'd met another woman or that he was freezing me out. But he didn't answer the door, even though his car was in the driveway. I waited, tried calling him, did everything I could to try and get his attention, but I got mad, thinking he was just ignoring me. So I looked in through the window and…that's when I saw that the place was a state. The place was turned upside down, furniture upturned, photographs smashed, a plate smashed on the floor. And I knew then that something was seriously wrong.

I called his work to see if they had seen him, but apparently, he hadn't been to work in days. Then I came straight here."

Olivia held her breath. Was this the man she was looking for? It sounded like it could be. They had been thinking they were looking for a woman, but it was definitely possible that the Gamemaster had misled them deliberately. Now, it seemed as though there was a possible candidate for their missing person.

"What did you say your partner's name is?"

"Garrett. Garrett Peabody," the woman said desperately. "Please, I know you're busy, but I know that something has happened. I tried the door, and it was left unlocked. He would never leave his door unlocked. And he's a very tidy person, he would never destroy his home like that. This happened days ago, I'm sure of it, and that's why he hasn't responded to me... please, you can't just turn me away."

"Alright, stay calm. Let's sit you down and get you a glass of water, you're clearly in distress. Then you can file a full report, and we'll see what we can do for you."

Olivia listened as their voices faded, the pair of them walking away together. Her shoulders relaxed a little. Garrett Peabody. They had a name. Olivia knew that they were supposedly meant to be looking for a woman, based on the voice note the Gamemaster had sent them, but Garrett's case fit the profile of everything else they were looking for. The timeline of his disappearance made sense, and with his girlfriend out of town, it had given the Gamemaster a window of opportunity to steal him away without anyone really noticing. It was the closest to a lead that they had been the entire week, and Olivia wasn't willing to let it go. Putting the clipboard aside, she rose to her feet and left the police station, hoping that all the time she'd spent there was about to pay off.

The moment she was outside, she took out her phone and dialed for Brock. He picked up moments later.

"Please tell me you've got something good. Today has been a total bust on my end," Brock said wearily.

"I think I might have something. A woman came in and reported her boyfriend to be missing. His name is Garrett Peabody. I know we were looking for a woman, but I think we might have been tricked. He fits the profile... he's not responded to texts for six days, and the woman was out of town, so she didn't know why he wasn't speaking to her. She said she went to his place today and found it trashed, and the door was left unlocked. She seemed to think that whatever had gone on there, it had happened at least a few days prior. And his car was still in the driveway... it all feels like it could make sense for who we're looking for. Oh, and she also said that she called his workplace, but they haven't seen him for days. It makes sense now that we haven't seen him reported as a missing person... his work clearly didn't report it, and his girlfriend wasn't around to know what was amiss."

"It does seem like this could be what we're looking for. God, I can't believe that the Gamemaster would be so sneaky... that voice note did seem too good to be true."

"We can't dwell on that now. We have to start making moves. We don't have much time left, and we need to find the victim before something awful happens. We still have no clue of where we can find him."

"The Gamemaster probably never expected us to figure out who her victim is. Maybe that'll work to our advantage. I'll bet that she cockily hid him somewhere obvious. Or at least obvious for the victim... I think we need to try and figure out if we can build a profile of who this guy is."

"Do we have time? We only have a few hours to figure out where to look for him."

"We'll just have to hope we can figure it out. I'll come and get you now. We'll do some digging to see if we can come up with something. You did good, Olivia, but this is far from over."

"I know," Olivia murmured. "This is only the start."

CHAPTER SEVEN

T HE MOMENT THAT OLIVIA AND BROCK WERE REUNITED, they didn't waste any time in digging for information about Garrett Peabody. But the challenge was, first of all, figuring out where to find him. Searching his name and St. Michael's on the internet brought up several results, which made the task a little harder than it should have been. Olivia had never imagined that there would be more than one person in the area with that name, but they had two options to look at. Both of whom had private profiles.

"Why does everyone set their social media profiles to private these days?" Brock muttered, his face screwed up in frustration. "It makes this so much harder."

"Probably because they don't want random people snooping on them. Although neither of these Garretts seems particularly of interest…ordinary guys living in an ordinary town, by the looks of them. I wonder what made the Gamemaster pick one of them as a victim…"

"At this point, it doesn't even matter that much. We just need to know which of them is the right one. Did you manage to glean anything about the girlfriend? Maybe that's the key. Did you get a name?"

"No… she didn't mention her name, or at least not that I had heard. I can remember what she looked like easily, but we can't even search through their friend lists to see if we can spot her." Olivia shut her eyes, picturing the woman in her head. "You know, she seemed familiar… like I've seen her somewhere before, and maybe recently." Olivia checked her watch. They still had a few hours before their midnight deadline, which was good, but not good enough. They needed to make some significant moves before things got worse. She thought back to her time at the town hall, taking part in local activities.

"Maybe I crossed paths with her while I was trying to get involved in the community…"

"Didn't you say she was out of town, and that's why she hadn't noticed that her boyfriend was missing?"

"Shoot, you're right. That's likely a dead end…"

"Hang on though. Maybe you didn't meet her…but perhaps you did see her at the town hall. Think about it…did you see any billboards, maybe? Maybe there was a local flier that had a picture of her in it, or maybe a photograph of her taking part in something? Maybe we should head to the town hall and see if we can spot something. It's better than scouring the internet when it feels like we're getting nowhere with it."

"Okay, I'm willing to give that a shot. I really do feel like I've seen her somewhere before…and my gut hasn't failed me today yet."

"It rarely does," Brock agreed, starting up the car. "Hopefully, it's not closed."

They arrived at the town hall just before eight. When they rushed up the steps to the building, the janitor was just closing up. He shook his head at Olivia and Brock as they made to enter.

"We close at eight."

"It's not eight yet," Brock said sternly. "Please, let us in, we will only be five minutes."

"Nah, man, I want to go home. I'm locking up now."

"Please! I left my phone here earlier, and I've only just been able to get back here," Olivia said, lying smoothly. "I'll be in and out… I know exactly where I left it."

The janitor wavered, looking irritable. But eventually, he sighed and ushered them inside.

"You've got exactly five minutes before I get mad."

"Thank you," Olivia said, pushing inside and breaking into a jog. Brock kept pace with her and let her lead him through the building to where the billboard was in the lobby. Olivia stopped and scanned the board, looking for the sight of the woman's familiar face.

"Describe her to me," Brock said, scanning the board too. Olivia frowned in concentration.

"She was short, plus-sized, with corkscrew-curled hair and pale skin. She was dressed well, clearly not short of money…"

"Is that her?" Brock asked, pointing to a photograph. The photo was of the members of the City Council and sure enough, Olivia spotted her right at the front, smiling widely.

"That's her! But we need a name…"

"It says on the plaque at the bottom… Sarah West. Maybe if we can search her up on social media, we might be able to figure out which Garrett she is in a relationship with. And then we'll have more to work with… maybe we figure out where he works and think of some places where he might have been taken."

"It's the best we've got."

"Hey! You said you'd be five minutes!" the janitor shouted after them. "Out!"

Olivia and Brock exchanged a quick glance with tired smiles as they headed for the exit. If time wasn't weighing down so heavily on them, Olivia knew they'd laugh about the grumpy janitor. But they couldn't afford even a moment of pleasantries. They headed straight back to the car, Olivia's fingers already tapping away on her phone as she looked up Sarah West.

"Here she is," Olivia said as she got into the car. "Quite active in the community and does a lot for this town. I guess maybe that's why her boyfriend tends to keep out of the public eye on his profiles... it keeps him out of the spotlight. But look... her profile shows him. . It's the second profile we looked at."

"Great. But we still don't know much about him. Just that he's a thirty-something man with a beard and poor fashion sense."

"Ouch. Harsh," Olivia teased gently. "But these photographs tell a bit of a story. He seems shy, kind of reserved in comparison to his girlfriend. There's not much about him on the internet, so it's kind of tough to get a read on him. But look here... she gets involved in all sorts of stuff. She went to the opening of a new store in the mall to cut the ribbon. He's in the background in uniform. Looks like this is where he works."

"Not just works... I think he owns the store," Brock said, showing Olivia something on his own phone. "Look at this article... *Garrett Peabody opens St. Michael's' brand new wellness store, the first in the area. The store offers vegan, healthy plant-based alternatives to many products in supermarkets. Garrett hopes to inspire the community to take their health more seriously, especially while maintaining a carbon neutral and environmentally friendly stance.*"

"Interesting... so maybe he's more present in the community than we originally thought. But yet somehow he's still been under the radar enough that he hasn't been reported as missing."

"I mean, a vegan alternative foods store is a bit niche. It might not be super popular, especially in a fishing town. Maybe he's sort of overlooked. Still, it is perhaps a little odd that no one realized he was gone."

"Is it possible that his store could be somewhere that the Gamemaster would hide him? It's like hiding him in plain sight, isn't it?"

"Although Sarah did say he hadn't been showing up to work…"

"But if he owns the place, that's not necessarily a cause for concern, is it? Plenty of people running a store don't work there every day. And the employees would be showing up regardless."

"So you think the Gamemaster has somehow managed to have him hidden there the entire time without anyone noticing?"

"Maybe? It's the kind of cruel trick that she would likely pull. That's assuming that she has taken him somewhere that he has a connection to. We're just speculating. But we only have a few hours left. We're going to have to hope we can find him somewhere that he has some kind of personal connection to. And if he's not at home…this is the closest thing we have to a reasonable answer."

"Alright. I guess we need to get to the mall then. And fast."

The mall was deserted. As Olivia and Brock parked outside it, she considered how they were going to get inside. It had likely been locked up hours ago when shopping hours came to an end. But they needed to get to the store and fast. There were only a few hours left before midnight, and if Garrett wasn't somehow hidden in his store, they'd need to try and find him elsewhere. Time was never on their side, but the looming deadline made Olivia's mouth feel dry and her heart speed up to a million miles an hour.

"Do we break in? Cause trouble and explain ourselves later?" Brock asked. "I mean, we might get ourselves into hot water, but it's worth it to save a life, right?"

"Maybe we won't need to," Olivia said, getting out of the car and approaching the building. Sure enough, as she walked up to the main doors, they opened for her automatically. A shiver ran down her spine. She had a distinct feeling that they were being watched. Like the Gamemaster had always planned for them to end up here.

"I think this is the right place," Olivia said quietly, ushering Brock forward. "We should be ready for anything."

"We're not even armed…"

"You heard the Gamemaster. We're not allowed to use anything we would normally have at our disposal. I'm pretty sure that includes guns."

"She's dangerous. We're walking into the lion's den. Are you sure it's worth the risk?"

"It has to be. If we don't follow the rules, he's going to die for sure."

"If the Gamemaster has somehow tricked us and we don't make it out alive…"

"Then we won't be around to complain about it," Olivia pointed out. "We're going in. It's the only way."

Brock hesitated for a moment and then followed her inside. The mall was dark, all of the lights switched off, but there was still a little natural light. Olivia used it to guide her way through the place, looking out for Garrett's store. They broke into a jog and Olivia's heart thudded in anticipation. She had no idea what they were about to see, but she was sure that nothing good would come from this trip to the mall.

Soon, she saw the sign for Garrett's wellness store up ahead. There was no light coming from inside the store, which somehow relieved Olivia. She was half expecting the Gamemaster to be there waiting for them, catching them off guard with no way to defend themselves. After all, when it came to the Gamemaster, rules were meant to be broken. But she kept moving anyway, determined that they would face their issue head on and not shy away. A man's life was at stake. That took priority over her own fear.

But as they turned into the store, a crude smell hit Olivia's nose, knocking her back a little. She blinked as she saw that something was dangling front and center in the middle of the shop.

The body of Garrett Peabody was hanging from the ceiling of the store. Olivia took a step back in horror. It wasn't yet midnight.

And yet there he was, strung up by his hands by two lengths of rope. It looked as though he must have been there a while. His body was eerily still, his chin tucked to his neck, eyes closed. And then it dawned on Olivia.

He was hung up like a puppet.

She was about to say something when she heard a crackle coming from further back in the store. That's when she noticed that the floor was wet and what the awful smell was. She grabbed Brock's hand as she saw the first flicker of fire roaring at the back of the store.

"It's a setup! We need to go!"

She pulled him away as fire began to roar all around them, catching on to the gasoline drizzled on the shop floor. The Gamemaster had fooled them twice in an instant. If they didn't run they'd be burned to a crisp.

She could feel heat licking at her back as they dove out of the store. Garrett—and everything he had built for himself—was engulfed by the fire in mere moments, the fire moving impossibly fast. Olivia spluttered as she and Brock ran from the mall. A fire alarm began to blare in their ears, dizzyingly loud. She had no time to consider what had happened, whether the Gamemaster had been waiting for them the entire time. She just ran until they made it outside to the open air, to relative safety.

Sweat was covering her face and her hands as she turned back to the mall, plumes of black smoke filling the mall. They'd been too late. They were supposed to have until midnight…

Or were they? The Gamemaster had never said anything about midnight. They had just assumed that was their deadline. If Garrett had been dead for some time, long enough for the Gamemaster to string him up that way, then when had their deadline been? That morning? A few hours ago? Olivia didn't understand. But then again, she knew better than to trust the Gamemaster, and she'd assumed the best from her anyway.

And now, a man was dead because of it.

CHAPTER EIGHT

OLIVIA COULDN'T SEEM TO GET HER HEART TO SLOW down. No matter how many deep breaths she took, she couldn't move past her anger at how they'd been lied to. Everything right from the start had been a misdirection—the time they were given, the voice note with the pleading woman, the expectations of the task at hand. All of it had been lies. And as a result, they had watched a dead man strung up right before their eyes.

No one deserved that kind of fate. When Olivia closed her eyes, she could imagine the burning flames licking at the man's hanging body in the middle of the store, skin melting away from his body as she ran for her own life, too late to save his. She had no idea what the man had done to be chosen by the Gamemaster. He was an ordinary shop owner with an ordinary life. He had a girlfriend who cared about him, probably friends and a family of some sort too. Now, his charred corpse was being fetched by the police as they spoke. People's lives would be destroyed, broken by the absence of him and the knowledge that he had died so horrifically. No one would understand why he had died, why he had been chosen to be killed in such a humiliating way.

Olivia and Brock included. They had been forced to leave it all behind, something Olivia rarely did. She always saw cases through to the end.

But with Garrett, she'd never stood a chance.

They were sitting in his car now, far enough away from the scene to not be spotted, but close enough to hear the sirens wailing as firemen and police flooded the area. Olivia's hands were shaking, and even Brock, putting his own hand over hers, couldn't stop them from trembling. They'd been lied to, of course. The voice note was never from the Gamemaster's victim, and that was the hardest thing to swallow. They had known that it was a possibility that they'd be lied to, but it had thrown them off course for the entire week. They'd been looking for a woman when the person in question was a man, and always had been. Olivia knew that given the right clues and being able to work with the police, things would have been much different. She was almost certain she could have saved the man if only they'd been given the right tools. Now, a life had been lost, and there was nothing that could ever change that.

But it was worse than just knowing a man was dead. Knowing that the Gamemaster had just set the tone for five weeks of hell. Another four times, they would have to repeat this process—a cold, terrifying process where they were constantly being misled and sent down the wrong path. Did that mean that they had to prepare themselves for four more deaths? Four more people being killed in cold blood, their lives snatched for them long before they'd been given a chance to save them.

Olivia hoped it wouldn't come to that, that the next one might be better, that they could learn from the mistakes they'd made this first time around. But even if they solved every case, she knew she would always live with the guilt of their failings that week. And perhaps that's exactly what the Gamemaster wanted. She might be in the process of leaving her life of crime behind, retiring early from her sickest games, but she was clearly making sure that she left some kind of awful legacy behind. Making sure that Olivia and Brock could never forget everything she had put them through.

How many lives had been affected by her now? How many more people would be hurt before it was all over? The pain was a rippling shockwave, starting with the dead and taking out all their loved ones in the process. Olivia didn't want to think about the hundreds of people that the Gamemaster had taken down. And as determined as she was to survive the torture she was being put through, it was weighing heavily on her heart.

She could tell it was bothering Brock, too. He looked exhausted and withdrawn, white-knuckled as he gripped the steering wheel of the stopped car. He let his shoulders slump forward and let out a long, drawn-out sigh.

"That was messed up."

Olivia nodded wordlessly. They didn't need to say out loud that there was no way they could go back there. They couldn't explain why they'd been on the scene without breaking the Gamemaster's rules or getting themselves into trouble. They were so deep in their lies now that they couldn't risk anyone else getting hurt, especially when it wouldn't do anyone good now. For Garrett, the worst had already happened. All they could do was move on and on to the next case, whether they liked it or not.

Sure enough, they soon received a call from Adeline. An unknown number popped up on Brock's phone, and it was obviously her. Who else would call him unexpectedly in the middle of the night? Olivia touched Brock's arm gently.

"Don't let her goad you. I know it's impossible. *She's* impossible. But don't let her win."

Brock looked as though he was about to argue, but then he nodded in understanding. As tempting as it was to give in to anger, they had to try and keep their cool. They couldn't let the Gamemaster keep winning against them.

Brock accepted the video call. Sure enough, Adeline's smug expression stared back at them, and she shrugged.

"Looks like you ran out of time. Sucks to be you. I guess you're really not all that much without all your weapons and support. That must be hard to swallow."

Neither Olivia nor Brock said a word. It was exhausting to speak to a woman like Adeline. There was no winning with her. She chuckled at their obvious discomfort as the silence stretched on.

"Well, not to worry. You'll have another few opportunities to redeem yourself before the end. And since it's midnight now, I can send you your next location and your next challenge. All will be revealed when you arrive in Riverside. But don't worry. I'll be nice this time. I'll let you work with the police."

"Really?" Olivia said, unable to keep the surprise out of her voice. "But why?"

"I guess I'm just feeling lenient! But be careful what you wish for, hmm? I think this case might rattle your bones even more than the last. I'm interested to see the outcome of this one."

"Do you ever let up?" Brock asked through gritted teeth. "Lives are at stake here. You're telling me you don't care at all?"

Adeline's head cocked to the side. "You're wrong about me, Brock. I do care. I'm just selective about what bothers me. And I think you'll understand me a whole lot better once we're done with the next challenge. I'll call you once you arrive at the location with more instructions. And trust me… this one you're going to want to solve. And fast."

CHAPTER NINE

OLIVIA AND BROCK MANAGED TO GRAB A FEW HOURS OF sleep between them as they took turns in driving to the next location. But as they arrived there, Olivia's eyelids were heavy. She knew she needed a proper rest if she was going to solve the mystery in time, but she was worried about what the outcome would be if she took precious hours to sleep. They knew now that there was a high chance that they would be faced with another impossible case, that no matter how many hours they put into it, it wouldn't be enough to save a life. Though Olivia was glad that they would be allowed to work with the police this time, she also felt like it had to be some kind of trick. Why would the Gamemaster suddenly change her mind? Was she bored at the possibility of them failing again, perhaps? Did some part of her want to see them succeed? She supposed they'd find out as soon as they were given their brief.

The Gamemaster called them mere moments after they crossed the city limits of Riverside. Olivia wondered how on earth she was keeping tabs on them, but she was sure that a criminal as established as the Gamemaster had her ways. It gave her the feeling of being watched, like the Gamemaster was sitting behind her in the car right then, only to disappear when she turned her neck to look. The thought was mildly horrifying, especially with a lack of sleep weighing her down. She had to blink several times to push away the sense of horror and dread.

Olivia picked up the call and faced off with the Gamemaster once again, expecting to see her smug face. But this time, Adeline Clarke looked stoic and serious. Gone was her smile and the sparkle in her eyes, replaced with something like maturity. It changed the planes of her face entirely. She looked older, somehow. Worn down. Olivia raised an eyebrow. Perhaps she had grown a conscience and realized that what she was doing was monstrous.

But somehow, Olivia doubted that.

"This challenge is a little different, and so are the rules as a result," Adeline said. "There's a missing girl. Eight years old…"

"You kidnapped a *child?*" Brock snapped in horror. Adeline scowled, genuinely seeming irritated at the accusation.

"Of course not. Who do you think I am?"

"You're a serial killer, Adeline. I wouldn't put anything past you. Don't act like you're some kind of saint whose word we can trust."

The Gamemaster scoffed. "Well, I'll have you know that I do have some lines I'm not willing to cross, whether you believe me or not. But you're not listening. I told you that this case is a little different. I didn't set this up myself. This girl has been missing for three weeks now. I keep seeing it on the news. There are a lot of people looking for this kid, but clearly they're not looking hard enough. I figured that while I'm warming you up for the main event, I'd send you to look for her. After all, you're supposed to be some of the best in the business. If anyone is going to find her, it's you."

Olivia blinked in confusion. Where had this all come from? She felt like this version of Adeline was a completely different woman from the one they'd spoken to only a few hours ago. What had changed in those restless hours Olivia had suffered through? She rolled her shoulders back, facing up to Adeline.

"And if we can't find her this week? What then? You're going to kill someone else to replace the girl? Or you'll find her yourself and kill her?"

Adeline rolled her eyes. "Don't be dumb. I'm not just going to kill some rando... that's not how these games work. And I don't want the kid dead. I just told you, I *want* you to find the girl alive and well. The next victim I have in mind for you... well, that's a different story. But I can do good deeds from time to time, and this is one of them. If you can find her and get her home to her parents, maybe I'll even give you some extra clues in the upcoming tasks. How generous is that?"

Olivia didn't know what to make of Adeline's apparent newfound heart. At least it confirmed one thing—they were right about her. She had a soft spot for children and their mothers. Or maybe even for women in general, though Olivia was less sure of that, given everything she'd been put through herself. The more they spoke to Adeline, the more Olivia was beginning to feel like she understood her and how to predict her moves, which was going to be the key to finding her and putting her back in prison. She hoped that might come in handy for the next few weeks. Maybe by the end of this nightmare, they might actually be able to take Adeline down once and for all.

"Well, I suppose you'd better brief us then. So we can get started," Brock said to Adeline. She scoffed.

"You're the ones who were so desperate to work with the police. So your wish is my command. You can go to the local station and ask the officers there what's going on. Flash your FBI ID, I'm sure that'll be enough to let you get involved. But maybe you can help this missing girl since the police here seem to be slacking."

"Why would you do this?" Olivia asked, her forehead creasing. "I don't understand what you're getting out of this. I thought you wanted to see blood spilled."

Adeline quirked a smile. "Don't try to put me into one of your little boxes, Olivia. I'm much more complex than you give me credit for. I might be a pain in your butt, but I do have a human side to me too. She's just a child. She shouldn't have to feel like she's been abandoned… like she's all alone in the world."

Interesting, Olivia thought to herself. Her words sounded as though they had weight to them. Olivia wondered if Adeline had ever felt alone in the world. Maybe it was because she'd always been different, full of violent thoughts and cruel tendencies. Or maybe she'd never really felt like she was cared about, as she had been abandoned by those supposed to take care of her. Was that why this case had piqued her interest? Was she hoping to resolve some of her own childhood trauma through the girl's case?

"Besides," Adeline continued. "Maybe I'll get something else from this whole experience. Something you haven't thought of. I guess it depends on the outcome of the case…"

"Stop speaking in riddles to us. Is this another one of your tricks?" Brock said wearily. "I don't believe for a second that you're actually sending us to do a good deed."

Adeline feigned hurt, clutching her heart theatrically. "You wound me so deeply, Brock. This is not a trick, I told you."

"You tell us a lot of things, and ninety percent of those things are absolute rubbish."

"Have a little faith. Every good villain has a weakness, right?" Adeline said lightly. "If the kid ends up dead, it'll only be because you don't get to her before her kidnapper does something. I won't touch a hair on her head. Now, get on with it and stop whining. It's getting annoying, and you're wasting time that could be spent looking for the child. I want to see how you handle this case. And I truly hope you figure it out."

Adeline ended the call before they could say anything else. Brock sighed, running a hand through his hair.

"She's always got a surprise up her sleeve, that one," he muttered. Olivia chewed her lip.

"She's slipping."

"How do you mean?"

"I don't know… she keeps showing her cards to us too plainly. I know she said she was getting tired, that she wants to finish all of this… but she's getting weirdly sentimental about stuff. I think she's having some kind of mental break. I mean, she's gone from murdering people at random to now trying to get us to save some random kid that she's been keeping tabs on. Surely this wasn't what she'd been planning all this time? All that stuff about the kid being alone in the world… I think she feels like she's got something in common with the missing girl. Like she feels like they're the same…"

"And by saving her, she's saving her past self? Something like that?"

"Yes, exactly! There's definitely something bigger going on here. It's influencing the way Adeline is playing the games. It's erratic and it probably makes her more dangerous… but it might also work in our favor, like this time around. I think if we can figure out what it is, we might be able to find her more easily, or at least decode these games she's setting up for us easier. I don't want to get my hopes up. I mean, we're still dealing with a psychopath. But maybe if we can poke and prod her a little… she might get closer to the edge."

"Close enough for us to give her a little push," Brock said darkly. Olivia shuddered ever so slightly.

"I wouldn't have put it like that... but if that's what it takes for us to save lives... then honestly, I'm willing to break her. She doesn't deserve our sympathy. So many have died at her hand."

"Hopefully, no more," Brock said gently, taking hold of her hand. "Let's find somewhere to get a few hours of sleep. In the morning, we'll get back to it. If the Gamemaster isn't going to kill anyone this time, then we can have a little time to recuperate. Otherwise, we're good to no one."

"Agreed. But I don't want to waste a single moment. Once we're rested, we're going looking for the girl. I just pray she's still alive."

The following morning, Olivia woke to Brock watching a video on his phone. She propped herself up on her elbow, glancing at his screen to see what he was doing.

"What's this you're watching?"

"An interview with the leader of the investigation of the missing girl," Brock told her. "The girl's name is Bethany Watson. She's been missing for three weeks now. She's Caucasian, blonde with blue eyes, from a middle-class background. Eight years old. Her parents are both teachers at the school that she goes to. I watched an interview with the pair of them... they both look absolutely harrowed by the whole thing."

"So we're not thinking they could be involved?"

"I don't think so. They have spent every waking hour searching for her, it seems. They've been running desperate campaigns looking for her, getting together search parties, going door to door to ask people questions and hand out posters... they don't seem like the kind to make their own child go missing."

"You're right, it doesn't sound very likely. Any possible suspects?"

"Not really. Adeline was implying that the police don't seem to be doing much, but this guy seems like he has his head screwed on. His name is Colton Wright, and he's been the chief of police in Jacobsville for the last ten years. He seems pretty committed to the search. I hate to say it, but it's likely the poor kid is dead at this point, or at least long gone from the area. If someone has taken her, they're not likely to stick around here waiting to be caught, are they?"

"Not with the scale of this current investigation going on. I guess we need to go and speak to Chief Wright and get some more information out of him if we can. If he's leading the investigation, maybe he has some things that he's not willing to admit in televised interviews. If we can pick his brains, it might help us get a grip on where to start."

"Hopefully, he'll let us help out. I mean, given that we're FBI, they could likely use some specialist insight right now. It's three weeks in now. They must be getting desperate."

Olivia and Brock didn't waste any more time. They rose, feeling a little refreshed from their brief rest, and headed out to the police station. As expected, when they arrived the place was buzzing with activity. Olivia was sure that they had as many officers as possible working on the case, even now that almost too much time had passed. Still, the place had a hopeful feel, and everyone seemed to be working hard. They didn't really pay much attention to Olivia and Brock as they tried to navigate their way inside. Olivia wasn't really interested in speaking to just anyone— she wanted the Chief. He was the heart of the investigation and their best chance of getting the case solved on the Gamemaster's tight deadline.

She spotted him in the thick of the crowd, talking to one of the other officers. He was a hulking figure, tall and broad, with white hair that stood out against tanned skin from many years out in the sun. He was frowning, and Olivia was sure that the case was taking a toll on the man in charge. She hoped that she could help him, that maybe he'd get some relief from assistance from the experts.

He looked up and caught her eye as they approached. He narrowed his eyes.

"Do I know you?"

"I don't think so," Olivia said, though she knew that often police officers and other law enforcement officials recognized her and Brock from their stint on the island. She had the Gamemaster to thank for that strange kind of fame in their community. "My partner and I heard about the case of Bethany Watson. We're part of the FBI and we'd like to help assist with your case."

Wright scoffed. "FBI? Here? You're kidding."

"Not at all," Brock said, showing Wright his badge.

"So you were sent here? I never got the memo."

Olivia was a little surprised by how defensive Wright seemed. Wasn't he glad to see them there, willing to help him with the case?

"We came ourselves. It's complicated," Brock said. "But we're here now and we would love to lend a hand, if we can. We just want to get Bethany home safe."

Wright sighed, running a hand through his gray hair. "Don't we all. It's been a mess over here... not a single clue as to where she's gone to. They tell you to follow the breadcrumbs, but something's scarfing them down before we can see them even for a second. There's no trail. And I'm sure you understand the implications of a long-missing person's case."

Olivia nodded grimly. "We do. But it's not always a death sentence. We have a week on our hands to help out... we were hoping that we can put it to use. Maybe we can offer a perspective that you haven't considered yet, or you might've missed. A fresh pair of eyes on a case can always be useful."

Wright put a heavy hand on her shoulder. "I appreciate what you're doing... but I assure you, we're looking down every avenue. My team has worked themselves to the bone. I know we're getting some bad press... people assume we're not trying hard enough. But that's not the case. And I don't think we need any more hands on this case."

"Please, sir. This isn't a time to push away help when it's offered," Brock insisted. "We know what we're doing. We've solved many cases about missing children. In fact, our first case together was a missing child's case. And guess what? Those girls came home. Those that we could save made it back. We can do the same for Bethany."

Wright wavered, glancing between the pair of them. Then he sighed. "You're right. We could use all the help we can get. I just don't know what else you can do for us…there are no prints on the scene, no signs of a struggle from the missing child, no nothing. We've looked a million times."

"Well, maybe we can take an extra look," Olivia said. "And I'd like to speak to Bethany's parents, if that can be arranged? I'm sure that will at least help fill us in on what's gone on here."

"Of course. I can send you to their house," Wright said encouragingly. "Take my number. I'll leave you to your own devices, but if you need anything, you can call my personal cell. I'll make sure I set you up where you need to be."

"Thank you. I think if we work together, we can find her. Whatever the outcome."

Wright nodded solemnly. "I certainly hope so."

CHAPTER TEN

OLIVIA AND BROCK TOOK WRIGHT'S NUMBER AND THE address to Bethany's parents' home, making their way over there immediately. They didn't talk much in the car. Normally, they'd have things to say to one another about the case, but the week ahead of them looked so grim that it didn't really bear thinking about it. A girl had been missing for three weeks. It was almost certain that she was dead. But somehow, the state of limbo—not knowing whether she was or wasn't—was worse. Olivia was almost glad that they only had a week to spend on the case, no matter the outcome. It was an awful thing to have to spend time working on, knowing that it so often ended in total devastation for families like Bethany's.

Wright had told them a little about Bethany's parents before they'd left—not only were they both teachers, but they were a young family, and they had raised her while training for their dream jobs. Tricia had taken some time out of work when Bethany was a baby and then returned to school with her as soon as she joined kindergarten. They were well-known in the community, and Bethany had a lot of friends at school. Her absence had been described as a crater in the town's workings. Olivia's throat had tightened when Wright told them that. The words were heavy and hard to take in. But it made her even more determined to find the little girl who had made such an impact on her community.

When they arrived at Bethany's home, Tricia and Tom were waiting for them, warned in advance of Olivia and Brock's arrival. Olivia could see how much weight they'd lost, both of them barely skin and bones, their eyes gaunt as they clutched one another like a lifeline. They only broke apart from one another to shake hands solemnly with Olivia and Brock.

"Thank you for coming to speak to us," Tom said gruffly, though his eyes shone with tears. "We're so grateful that this is being taken so seriously as to involve the FBI...we're getting desperate here."

"We're here to help in any way we can," Olivia said gently.

"Please come inside and take a seat. Can I make anyone some tea?" Tricia asked in a trembling voice. Olivia shook her head.

"That's okay. Let's get right to it, shall we?"

They sat in the living room, Olivia and Brock opposite Bethany's parents on a small loveseat. They once again joined hands, gripping one another with weary desperation.

"So. From what we know, this is the first disappearance of its kind in this town?" Brock asked. Tricia nodded.

"We don't get much going on around here...which is why we were so horrified when this happened. We put Bethany to bed as normal three weeks ago... and when we got up in the morning, she simply wasn't there. The police searched the house for signs of what might have happened... we couldn't understand how we could sleep through someone breaking into our home and taking our baby girl away..." Tricia shook her head. "It's been hell. We never imagined... we never thought something like this could happen to us."

"You said the police were thorough in their search?" Brock pressed. Tom nodded.

"We watched them do it. They had so many people coming through this house, looking for hairs, fingerprints, signs of disturbances... but that was the thing. Everything felt completely normal the morning we woke up. Nothing seemed out of place. The only sign she was gone was her unmade bed, left the way it had been when she was... taken. And no, we don't think she ran off. We were asked that so many times... but we have a good relationship with our daughter. And she would be too frightened to do something so bold. I don't think she would know how to get out of the house alone. And... and all of her shoes were left in her closet... it was like she just disappeared into thin air."

Olivia nodded sympathetically. She could only imagine the agony they were feeling—the agony they held for all to see on their faces. They were haunted by it, even if their daughter might still be alive. Still, they hadn't lost hope. She admired that.

"Did you have any feeling that this was coming before it happened?" Brock asked gently. "Any indicators that something was going on?"

"We've seen a few... strange things in the neighborhood," Tricia admitted. "In our own backyard, actually."

"Someone tried to break in?" Brock asked, frowning. Tricia shook her head.

"No, not exactly. I was going to bed one night and as I went to close the curtains... I saw a figure standing in the garden. They had binoculars, I was sure of it. I thought maybe someone might be trying to spy on me getting changed or something to that effect. But after Bethany disappeared, I began to consider...

that someone might be looking out for an opportunity to steal our child away. I felt it had to be connected. But though I swear I saw the figure twice... I was the only eyewitness, and I never had enough evidence to find someone. In the dark—it was very late both times I saw the person—I couldn't tell much about the person, and they left no trace behind. Tom ran outside to face them, but they were always gone before he got to them." Tricia swallowed, sniffing a little as her eyes welled with tears. "The week that Bethany disappeared, we were starting to speak with a security company about getting cameras installed. But by then, we were too late. We had hoped we might capture an image of whoever was coming into our property... but the night it all happened, we didn't hear or see a thing. And believe me, we've been on high alert, checking our doors and windows... we were going to have the whole house kitted out just in case. But it was too little too late."

"You can't blame yourself. For someone to come inside your home and kidnap your child without any way of being detected... they must have known exactly what they were doing," Olivia said. "I presume you reported to the police when you saw the person out there?"

"Yes. Both times. But without any evidence of what happened... the police had little they could do about it. But I don't feel like we were taken very seriously... at least not until her actual disappearance. And I wonder if... if they'd listened earlier..."

"Stop torturing yourself, babe," Tom soothed, squeezing his wife's hand. "It's not our fault. Some sicko did this. That was always out of our control."

"Has anyone taken any kind of... special interest in Bethany?" Olivia asked delicately. Tricia frowned, looking mortified.

"Special interest?"

Olivia always hated addressing the possibility of child sexual abuse, especially to the parent of a missing kid. But it had to be brought up, though Tricia seemed horrified and confused about the line of questioning. Surely she'd been asked this question in the last three weeks? Had no one considered that the person who took Bethany might have such dark impulses?

"I hate to ask ... it's just that an adult kidnapping a child often has ... a sexual interest in them. Either that or some kind of interest in being a parent to the child. I know that's an awful thing to have to consider, and it might make you uncomfortable to think about. But anything you can tell us might help us in the search for your child. Has anyone in the community ever seemed inappropriately interested in Bethany? Perhaps they're overly friendly, or maybe they have tried to form a strong bond with her in some way? One of the other teachers at the school, maybe?"

"Absolutely not!" Tom said, looking appalled. "No one at work has ever been inappropriate with Bethany."

"We don't mean to imply that they have," Olivia said calmly. "We're just asking about possibilities where an older person, maybe someone with some authority, might have been in a position to get closer with your daughter. Think hard."

Tricia glanced anxiously at Tom for a moment, looking a little guilty, like she was holding something back. Olivia leaned forward.

"Tricia?"

She sighed, bowing her head ever so slightly.

"I might ... I might regret saying this. He seems like a decent man, for the most part. But ... we have a young priest at our local church. He's only in his mid-twenties, not much younger than we are ... and he has always made me a little ... uncomfortable."

"He's very ... enthusiastic," Tom said, squirming a little. "We used to go to church regularly, but since he took over, we've felt as though we'd rather keep our distance. He just seems a bit too into it, you know?"

"But that's just how we feel," Tricia said quickly. "We wouldn't want to imply that there's something wrong with him ... a lot of people in this town appreciate him. He's just not for us ... and Bethany seemed uncomfortable about him. He was always just a bit ... friendly. Familiar, you know? He always called us his family, and he likes to hug the kids, give them sweets, encourages them all to go to Sunday school…"

"It was all just too much," Tom said with a decisive nod. "So we stopped going. He might not particularly have focused on Bethany more than the other kids, but I'm just not totally sure about him. He sort of pushes boundaries." Tom swallowed, looking guilty. "We don't want to throw anyone under the bus… he could just be a nice man trying to interest kids in God. But he's the person that comes to mind when you mention… inappropriate behavior."

Olivia nodded. "Understood. It's okay. You have to follow your gut. If you feel like it's worth our time to speak to him then we certainly will. We're willing to try any avenue to get you answers."

"Thank you," Tricia said tearfully, gripping her husband's hand tightly. "We're glad you came… we know that the police are doing their best, but we're so anxious to have our baby home… and it feels like this case isn't moving anywhere."

"You seem to be asking the right questions. Things they didn't come up with themselves… we never even considered the possibility of something so… sinister being involved," Tom said. His throat sounded like it had closed up, his words barely choking their way out. A tear ran down his cheek. "We just want her back safely… we can't even comprehend what might have happened to her. It's too much."

"We hope we can bring you good news," Olivia said carefully. She didn't want to promise them anything when she knew how likely it was that their daughter was already dead. But that didn't mean she had given up on the case. And whether they knew it or not, Bethany's parents had given them something good to work with. The priest sounded like a likely candidate. She didn't want to *hope* it was him, but she also wanted to find answers, and quickly. For the sake of Bethany's parents, and Bethany herself. If she was still alive, she certainly wasn't safe.

CHAPTER ELEVEN

THE CHURCH WAS NEARLY FULL WHEN OLIVIA AND BROCK arrived. A service seemed to have just begun, and there was music coming from inside, soft and melodic. But, after the accusations from Tricia and Tom, Olivia didn't feel particularly safe sitting inside the church. She and Brock remained at the back, watching the service unfold.

The church was half full, quite a feat for a modern church, Olivia thought. She'd never been religious herself, but she knew that the church near where she'd grown up had often been mostly empty. Many places now struggled to fill the pews in their churches.

But Olivia could see the appeal of the priest, Father Green. He wasn't much younger than she was, likely in his late twenties. He was handsome in a stripped-back kind of way, his dark hair and shining blue eyes not unpleasant on the eye, and he brought a little flair to the service that had the churchgoers on their feet. He had them singing modern songs about God, making the kids at the church giggle, and he made jokes between each of his sermons. He was adapting his service to fit the needs of the modern Christian. In any other circumstances, Olivia felt she would be impressed by this.

But she had to take Tricia and Tom's concerns seriously. While they hadn't expressed exactly why Father Green made them uncomfortable, they had definitely felt some need to bring up his name in conversation. Olivia wouldn't feel as though she was doing her job until she fully investigated the man and what he brought to the community.

When the church began to clear, Olivia and Brock stayed close to the door, watching as Father Green dismissed his congregation. He spoke to every single person at the door, giving the children high fives, thanking their parents for their generous donations to the church, saying prayers for loved ones who hadn't made it to church that day for various reasons. Watching him, Olivia almost felt guilty for having to approach him about something so terrible. But she also knew that sometimes, the least likely candidates were capable of the most terrible things. He might seem like a good man in his comfort zone, surrounded by people who trusted and loved him. But Olivia knew that his attitude might change once they started questioning him and putting him in an uncomfortable position. They had to be prepared for any possibility.

As the last person filtered out of the door, Olivia and Brock stepped up to greet the priest. He looked a little surprised to see new faces in the room, but his eyes lit up as he greeted each of them with a handshake.

"Hello there. I don't think I've seen you here before. Are you new to town?" Father Green asked pleasantly. Olivia winced. He really was sugar-sweet, and it wasn't going to be easy to wipe that smile off his face.

"Actually, no. I'm Olivia Knight, this is my partner, Brock Tanner. We work for the FBI... and we're currently helping with the investigation of the missing girl."

Father Green's smile faded a little. "Ah, yes, young Bethany. Such a sweet child. Quiet, but very sweet. And her parents must be just devastated. I don't know if I can really help you if that's what you're hoping for, though. The family stopped coming to church a while back. No hard feelings on them, of course. Everyone explores their faith in their own way. But I have to admit, I haven't even seen them around much. If you have any questions, though, I'll do my best to answer them."

"Well, this isn't easy to say, Father Green, but Tricia and Tom did mention that they had a reason for not continuing to bring Bethany to the church. They said... they said that they felt a little uncomfortable since you took over at the church."

Father Green blinked several times. "In what way?"

"They didn't go into too much detail. But they implied that perhaps you're... overenthusiastic. And I wonder if perhaps that has led them to wanting to keep Bethany away."

Father Green's eyes turned cloudy with hurt. He ran a hand through his hair, clearly uncomfortable.

"Well I... I simply don't know what to say. I never intended to make anyone feel like they can't come to church... I admit I have changed things a lot around here. I used to come to the church to see what I was working with before I took over... it was the same handful of older people attending every day, listening to boring sermons and singing the same hymns over and over... my intention was always to modernize the church and try to get the younger generation involved more. In case you haven't noticed, religion isn't really considered cool with the kids... but I hoped I was changing that. I had no idea that Tricia and Tom left because of me. I just don't really understand what I did wrong..."

"We're just working with the information that we have," Brock said reassuringly. "We have to be thorough in our search for Bethany and your name was mentioned."

Father Green's eyes widened. "So you're investigating me?"

"We just want to talk to you."

Father Green's eyes were distant now, his expression full of fear. "Where did I go so wrong? I have never, *ever* intended harm to anyone. I love my job. I love my community, my flock. But these baseless accusations... where have they come from? Is it because I try to get the kids involved? The new songs, the high fives? I'm just trying to stay relevant... is that so wrong?"

"Don't spiral, Father. No one is accusing you directly. Like we said, this is just a conversation we're having here. If you have nothing to hide then you have nothing to fear," Olivia said pointedly. She wanted to believe that this seemingly kind priest hadn't done anything wrong, but his intense response to their questioning definitely hinted at something being amiss.

Father Green lowered himself into one of the pews, his eyes still glassy.

"I feel... I feel hurt. Bethany was a lovely young girl. I would never do anything to endanger her or to hurt her family. Though they have wounded me, I would never wish any harm on them," Father Green said with a sniff. "I know that some people may find me intense, and I can understand that I don't appeal to everyone who used to come to church here. But I am a true man of God. I would never go against his will, and I would never harm another living creature. Though I myself suffered as a boy, I would never wish that on anyone else. The papers say that Bethany was likely taken by someone with... nefarious intentions. To think that Bethany might be suffering the way that I did... it's unspeakable."

That captured Olivia's attention even more. She slipped into the pew in front of Father Green's, putting a gentle hand on his arm.

"You were abused?"

Father Green flinched a little as though he hadn't meant to open up so much in front of them. But he didn't move away from Olivia's comforting hand.

"Yes."

"By... by someone in this community?"

"Yes," he whispered. "But... I was never able to name who did it to me. They were taken into custody for a time, but I was too afraid then to come forward with what I knew. The trauma has kept me silent all these years. The person in question walks free, even now. I've always wished to have the courage to move past that mental block... to see clearly the person who hurt me and to name them. But too much time has passed, and I am weak."

"Not weak. Afraid, and there's no shame in that," Olivia told him gently. "But whatever you can tell us... it could help save Bethany. If the person who hurt you is still walking free... perhaps they are doing the same thing to her now. You couldn't stop it from happening to you as a child. But you might be able to save someone else from the same fate."

"I... I can't speak plainly."

"Then tell us in riddles. Let us take it from there," Olivia insisted. She would rather be given half-truths than silence. Father Green swallowed and nodded, his expression plagued with fear. Gone was the confident man from his service minutes earlier. Now, he was a broken young man, unable to speak his truth.

"I carry the burden of many secrets in this church. Confessions," Father Green whispered. "Confessions that make my skin crawl. But I cannot speak up. It is against my oath. And it's dangerous. People would die if I told you more."

"You've been threatened?"

Father Green lowered his head. "This town is plagued with evil. I am supposed to be a beacon of safety... but we are never truly safe. Not even in the hands of people who are meant to protect us." His eyes met Olivia's. "The apple never falls too far from the tree, Olivia. Remember that. And remember that a library often holds all of the answers."

Before Olivia could ask what he meant, Father Green stood up, his head lowered to his chest once again.

"I'm sorry, but that is all I can say. I hope you find the child. And I hope that when you do… perhaps I will be free too."

Olivia allowed him to walk away, though she wished she could delve much deeper. But after seeing the fear in his eyes, she knew that pushing Father Green would only make things worse for him, and they wouldn't be any closer to the answers. Olivia turned to Brock.

"I guess we need to pay a visit to the library then."

The local library was small, but Olivia felt confident about what they might find there. It was also pretty much empty, so she and Brock had the place to themselves.

"I think we should be looking at the newspaper archives," Olivia whispered, feeling the need to keep her voice low. Not just because they were in a library but in case anyone heard what they were looking for and became suspicious of them. "We need to look at the years when Father Green was a child and find out what happened to him. He said his abuser was never named and that they were let go… but he also said that the apple doesn't fall far from the tree. Perhaps whoever we're looking for has a son or daughter in the town who might be capable of something so awful… it seems like that was what he might be implying, anyway."

"We'll need more than one testimony to pin this, though. Father Green's abuse was brushed aside. Whoever hurt him likely had some power that kept them from being affected. The same might be said for their family member."

"I know. It could all be one big long shot. But it's got to be worth a try. We might save more than one person with this investigation… this could heal the town too."

The archives smelled of ink and old paper. The newspapers weren't in great condition, practically crumbling as Olivia picked them up to flick through, but there were secrets concealed between the pages. Olivia felt hopeful as she looked through the pages of the papers from twenty years before.

"We're going to have to look over quite a long time span," Olivia said. "We don't have Father Green's exact age, and we don't know how old he was when he suffered the abuse. If neither he nor his abuser were named in the papers, it's going to be even harder to find what we're searching for."

"I think we can narrow it down a little," Brock said. "Bethany is eight years old. If we assume the abuser is either the same person or related to Father Green's abuser, then we can come to the conclusion that they have a… type. Bethany is old enough to be aware of what is happening to her, at least on some level. Father Green seems to remember his own trauma very well, and he can articulate about it on some level. To me, it seems as though we're looking for someone who had an unhealthy obsession with young children, but not toddlers or babies. Children who would be present in the abuse." Brock swallowed, looking disgusted. He shuddered and then continued. "From this, we can probably narrow it down to around five years… to account for the age Father Green is now and how old he would've been during the abuse. So when we think he was around seven or eight, which would've been twenty years ago, give or take a few years. I think we're looking for the late nineties, early two-thousands."

"You're right. Good thinking," Olivia said. "Let's focus there first then."

It was a long process. Olivia tried searching online for the newspapers, hoping they might be backdated that far and they'd be able to search by keywords, but she had no luck. That meant going through every page of every paper laboriously, hoping for some sign of the abuse that Father Green had alluded to. Olivia's heart was thudding hard as she flicked through the pages. Every moment that passed was another moment where Bethany was in the hands of someone cruel and cold, someone who was likely willing to hurt her for their own sick needs. She didn't want to waste a single moment of time.

Her breath hitched as she reached for the next paper. The headline news caught her eye.

"Brock, look at this. *Local police officer, accused of the unthinkable, released from custody today.*"

Brock dropped his own article to join Olivia at her side. She cleared her throat and began to read it aloud in a whisper.

"Our once peaceful town has been shaken up by a child's need for attention and an accusation destined to destroy a man in uniform's reputation. For the last three days, the police station has been in lockdown while the officers completed a thorough in-house investigation of one of their own, following a child's cry for help to a teacher at school. Accused of abuse, the officer in question has now been discounted as a suspect, leaving the community feeling safer once again. But the question is still up in the air; what would make a child cry wolf over something so serious? The child, only seven years of age, reportedly discussed in detail with the police the supposed abuse they received from a member of the police, but with no physical evidence to support the claim, the report was retracted on the third day of questioning. The officer, unnamed for his own protection, has been released without being charged due to lack of evidence. The child, also unnamed, will be referred for intense therapy to recover from these unfounded accusations. The parents of the child will also be under investigation to try and figure out where the child might have come up with such tall tales from."

Brock shook his head in disgust. "Clearly it was covered up. What reason would a child have to lie about something so awful? Most children wouldn't even know how to lie about such a subject… sexual abuse isn't something children know about unless they have experienced it."

"It's certainly not an ordinary accusation to make," Olivia agreed. "And the way it was investigated *in house?* The other officers clearly covered for the officer who hurt Father Green. I can't imagine how awful that would have been for him ... growing up knowing that there's no justice in a town like this."

"And now history is likely repeating itself," Brock growled. "No wonder Father Green was terrified to speak up. We can't just let this go. We need to turn our attention toward the police."

"But how? If we show that we're suspicious, we might cause more problems. And besides, there may still be officers on the squad who helped with the cover-up. They'll go to their graves swearing that they were doing the right thing."

"Then we will have to be more subtle than that. We need to know more about every officer who has served in the last twenty years. And if there are family ties in the police, that would be even better. Then we can make sense of what Father Green meant when he said the apple doesn't fall far from the tree."

"We're going to have to be careful. We could easily get into trouble if we're poking in all the wrong places. I'm beginning to understand why the Gamemaster let us talk to the police. This must go so much deeper than we first thought ..."

Olivia's eyes darkened. "There's a child's life at stake here. Screw it if we get into trouble. We have to do the right thing."

CHAPTER TWELVE

"WHERE DO YOU THINK WE SHOULD START WITH THE police?" Olivia asked as she and Brock settled down for an evening of investigations in their poky hotel room. There hadn't been many choices of places to stay the night, but Olivia didn't even mind the yellowed sheets and the distinct smell of cigarettes resting in the air. She didn't plan to do much sleeping anyway.

"I guess everyone is a suspect right now," Brock said with a sigh. "But if we're looking for someone with a son or daughter in the force, then that narrows down our search a lot. The apple doesn't fall far from the tree… that sounds like the key to what we're looking for with this. Assuming that Father Green's words hold some truth."

"I don't see why he would be so vague if he wasn't actually scared," Olivia said. "If he was just trying to protect his own skin, he would've started pointing fingers a lot more directly. He seemed genuinely upset with the accusation against him… and to be honest, he seemed like a good man. He clearly cares for his congregation.. I think we can put suspicions of him to one side and work with what he told us."

"Okay, let's say we do that. How are we going to investigate the police without them cottoning onto us? We can't really afford to upset anyone if we want to be kept on the case, so we're going to need to be careful."

"Agreed. Maybe for now we'll just have to work with what we can online. Maybe the Jacobsville PD website will have a photograph of all of the officers, or some kind of history about who has worked there. That will help us determine if there are any family ties in the place to look into further."

"Okay, cool. I guess that's where we start then."

Olivia got out her laptop and handed it over to Brock so that he could get them set up while she made them both a coffee. When she sat down beside him at the small table provided in their room, she saw that he had found the police station's website. And sure enough, there was a handy little profile about each of the officers. First up with Chief Colton Wright, his photograph staring back at them sternly. He kept his chin high and even in the photograph, he had an air of dominance.

"He's obviously well respected at the station," Brock said, hovering over his photograph. "And he's worked his way up to the top."

"It's not a huge station to work at," Olivia pointed out, scrolling through the other officers. Their names and faces didn't mean much to her yet—they hadn't met anyone other than Wright at the station. "Interesting… seems like it's an all-boys club in this place. There's only one female officer."

"Hm. A lot of small towns tend to be that way…they hold their values in such a tight-knit community. I'm not sure it's anything to read into."

"Well, we're here for the family ties, so I guess we can leave that for now. Do we have any name matches, or family resemblances?"

"Let's have a proper look…oh, there we are. There's a Leon Benson, and an older gentleman, Frank Benson. According to the profile, Frank retired four years ago… but he was active in the force during the time we're investigating. He could definitely have been involved in what happened to Father Green."

"Well that's definitely worth investigating then. Are there any others? I suppose there could be changes to names through marriage and such, but with all of the officers being men, I guess they're more likely to have kept their father's names…"

"Oh God… is that Colton's father?"

Olivia lost her train of thought at Brock's outburst. She stared at the screen, where there was a picture of the retired officer, Ron Wright. The family resemblance was certainly there, and there was a similarly cold expression resting on his face. Olivia took a steadying breath.

Brock shook his head after a moment. "This is a little far-fetched even for us… are we really considering that the lead officer on this investigation could be involved in Bethany's disappearance?"

"Brock, we can't discount it and you know it. We always knew we were going to have to dig in on *someone* on this police force. Why not the lead of the investigation? He's the one with the control. Isn't it possible that he's using that as a way to keep everyone else off the scent? I mean, he hasn't got anywhere in the last three weeks of investigation. I wonder why that could be…"

"It feels wrong to even think that he's the one responsible for this…it's so cold and cruel, to deliberately mislead everyone… to steal a child away right under her parent's noses… it's a bold move."

"It is, but not impossible. It depends how much evil we believe is possible," Olivia said with a raised eyebrow. They were no stranger to bad people. Olivia didn't see why Brock was finding this such a hard pill to swallow. It wouldn't be the first child kidnapper they'd dealt with. In fact, their very first case together had been along a similar vein. What was so impossible about it happening again?

"Time isn't our friend here," Olivia reminded Brock. "We really can't afford to *umm* and *ahh* based on our first impressions of a man we don't know. Colton is as much a suspect as Leon and Frank Benson. If we're going with the family connections, those are our two sets of suspects. We have to look into both, and fast."

Brock hesitated a moment before nodding. "Alright. I suppose you're right. Where do you want to start?"

"With Wright, for sure. Either he's involved or this is happening under his watch. Either way, I think he has a role to play in this, and he can't be overlooked. Plus, we know a little about him. It'll make it easier to start off with him. Let's see it as a process of elimination. If we don't find any dirt on him, then we can go all in with Leon and Frank."

"Alright, you're the boss. What are we looking for, then? How do we connect Wright and his father back to Father Green and Bethany? Or just one or the other for now?"

"I'm not sure yet. The newspaper articles didn't give too much away about the police officer who was under investigation. They did their best to keep it all under wraps and keep everyone anonymous. That's surely the only way the town has moved on from such an accusation. But whoever it was kept their job, so it could be either of the older men."

"But it's the sons we're looking at for Bethany's disappearance, most likely," Brock reminded her. "So if we're looking into Wright, we have to know more about him."

"Alright, I guess we're doing some internet surfing then. You check out his socials. I'll see if I can find any articles about cases he's worked on or local news about his life. Small towns love reporting on the small stuff. I bet we can glean quite a lot without having to alert Wright to what we're up to."

"Let's hope so. Because if we're wrong about this, he's going to kick us off the case the moment he finds out what we're doing."

"Then we'll be extra careful," Olivia said. "We've got one shot at this. We can't afford to mess it up."

The pair of them got to work. It didn't take long for either of them to find out more about him. Brock found his social media profiles right away, but he seemed to be a closed book—aside from pictures of him and his father catching big fish together, there wasn't much about Wright as a person. He didn't post very often, but he was often tagged in posts by others in the community—most of them middle-aged women thanking him for helping them around the town. But, there was one thing that interested both Olivia and Brock.

"Hmm. Looks like he's married," Brock said, showing Olivia the screen. "But it doesn't say to whom."

"Perhaps I can find something about it in a local news article," Olivia mused, searching Wright's name and *marriage* into the search engine. After filtering by their location, Olivia came up with an article.

"Local police captain marries," Olivia read out loud. "This was nine years ago. It says that he married his high school sweetheart, Terri Gladstone. They had a pretty big ceremony, the whole town was invited to get involved, and they had a bit of a street party… so it's kind of interesting that there's no trace of her on socials, right?"

"Looks like she skipped town a while back," Brock said as he continued his investigation on the laptop. "Look at this article… *well-loved nail technician closes up her store, leaving five employees without work.* It goes on to say that Terri was well known in the community and that the business was doing really well, but she decided to shut down her business without warning five years ago. She left town without really saying anything to anyone."

"Why on earth would she do that?" Olivia wondered aloud. "It sounds like she had a good setup here… unless the marriage fell apart? But why is Wright still presenting them as married, then? It's been five years. Surely she would've filed for a divorce by now? Unless there's some part of the story that we're missing…"

"Maybe he's trying to pretend like nothing ever happened… but if she's not in town, then where is she? How does Wright explain that one to people when they ask?"

"We need to find her and speak to her," Olivia said. "If she ran away for a good reason, then we need to know about it. It might unveil something about Wright that we haven't figured out yet. Maybe it's all perfectly innocent. Maybe she just needed to get out of this town. But it all feels a bit too strange to blow it off, especially given that we're looking for a man who could be capable of really terrible things. If she was aware of any bad blood in the family, it's no wonder she got out of Dodge."

"It takes a lot to make a person uproot their life like that," Brock agreed. "She must have been really scared or worried to just leave without giving anyone a reason."

"First thing tomorrow, we'll go and find her," Olivia said. "If anyone knows the nature of Wright, it will be his estranged wife. It sounds like she got up and left as quickly as she could. Happy people don't do that. Whatever happened between her and Wright, it sounds like it was a bit of a mess. Maybe she can tell us more about him."

Olivia and Brock managed to track Terri Wright to a small town a few miles away. It had taken quite some digging to figure out where she was, and Olivia knew that was likely deliberate. They were fortunate that she was still close enough for them to get in touch with her easily. They arrived at nine am and found that there was a car parked outside her house. They wasted no time in hanging around, heading up to her door and knocking right away.

It was a while before they heard shuffling behind the door. Olivia waited, wondering what was taking so long for the woman to show up. Then she spotted the peephole in the door. She wondered if Terri was a little paranoid, trying to spy on who was at the door before opening it up. Olivia frowned at the thought. How badly had leaving Wright messed her up?

Olivia knocked a second time.

"Terri Wright? We're with the FBI. We'd like to talk to you about something very serious. A missing child," Olivia said through the door. She knew Terri was on the other side, listening, weighing up whether she should open the door. If Terri had suspicions about her husband being corrupt, then Olivia knew there was no good reason for Terri to trust them either. She knew that being in the police didn't mean that someone was a good person. But Olivia needed her to trust them, at least temporarily. They had to expose the rot within Bethany's hometown.

"We don't mean to bother you," Brock continued. "It's just that we need to speak to you about your husband, Colton Wright."

"He's not my husband," a small voice said from inside. "Well… I suppose he is. But not in any of the ways that matter."

"Then perhaps you can help us out by explaining why that is," Olivia said gently. "I'm sorry to come to your home like this, but this is important. A young girl is missing and we're investigating the police. We have heard rumors of previous incidents… a police officer years ago attacked a child. And now we think it's happening again. We have reason to believe there are two people involved… perhaps a father and son. Would you know anything about that, Terri?"

There was a long silence before the door finally creaked open a few inches. Around the door, a mouse-like face appeared. The woman was petite with dirty blonde hair. She looked tired and worried, but it looked as though she might have been that way for a long time.

"Are you alone?" she whispered, her eyes darting around. "I'll need to see some credentials…"

"We're alone. No one knows we're here," Brock assured her, producing his badge for her to see. "And we're on your side. We just want to hear your story."

Terri hesitated another moment before fully opening the door to allow them to step inside.

"Quickly. Before someone sees you."

The house was small, but clean and homey. There were a lot of photographs in the living room of Terri and a young girl, both of them smiling brightly. And all of a sudden, something hit home for Olivia.

Terri had a daughter.

Colton's daughter.

And now it made sense why she had run away all of a sudden. Terri knew something about Colton's nature, Olivia was sure of it. Not to mention that Colton's father was the grandfather of her child. Terri clocked Olivia looking at the photographs and swallowed.

"I wondered if this day would come," Terri whispered. She walked to the sofa and lowered herself into it slowly, as though her legs were about to give out. "I wondered when the past would catch up to me."

"You know why we're here, don't you?" Brock asked. Terri nodded.

"I've been watching the news. I've seen my husband leading the investigation looking for that poor girl… and I've stayed silent. Because I had to. He's kept me quiet for years."

"Why don't you tell us everything from the beginning?" Olivia said softly. "We need to know it all."

Terri put a hand to her throat, looking pained.

"You have to promise that my daughter will be safe. She's at school right now… if I tell you everything, will you make sure that she's okay? That nothing happens to her, no matter how your investigation plays out?"

"Of course we will," Olivia soothed. "Your daughter will be our priority as much as finding Bethany. We won't allow anything to happen to her."

Terri's shoulders deflated. "Okay. I can tell you everything. I've lived for so many years in fear... it feels good to know I can finally tell someone. I've wanted to go to the police for so long... but with Colton having everyone in Jacobsville under his thumb, I've never known who I can trust. And he told me that he would kill me if I ever exposed him for what he is."

"You left your home five years ago, is that correct?"

Terri nodded. "Colton is the only man I've ever loved. We were high school sweethearts. I couldn't believe my luck when he chose me, back then. None of the other boys at school were interested in me... I had a body like a boy back then and a baby face. The boys would tease me endlessly, and I was sure that I'd never find a boyfriend. But Colton liked me as I was. And it wasn't until later on, when my body changed and I filled out that I understood why... he liked me child-like. It was his way to hold back his... urges, I suppose. It was toeing the line, I guess, because of course I was his age... there was nothing wrong with our relationship at the time. But like I said... my body changed. I began to show my age. And then I got pregnant with our daughter and everything was just... different."

Olivia's skin was crawling. *This poor woman,* she thought.

"Did you begin to worry? About what your husband was truly interested in?"

Terri swallowed. "It was after our daughter was born that my fear intensified. I thought I was going crazy... but I always felt that he looked at her with too much... love. Except it wasn't love. You know what I'm getting at, don't you? I tried to explain my feelings to my girlfriends, but they thought I was crazy. I was diagnosed with postpartum depression, but I knew it wasn't that. I wasn't depressed, I was afraid. I tried everything to get our marriage back on track. I was obsessively undereating, trying to get my body to how it had been before, hoping to distract his focus. But in the meantime, I couldn't let him be alone with our child. It scared me to no end. And nothing worked. He began to treat me like some disgusting creature, like he'd never had love for me in his life. And my realizations became more and more clear. He'd loved me when I was a child. And now he was setting his sights elsewhere."

Terri took a deep breath, trying to compose herself. Olivia felt horrified by the story, not knowing how to respond to the woman's clear grief of the life she'd lived. Olivia could see how the fear had twisted her entire being. And now, she was having to relive it all, knowing that she had been alone in her fears for such a long time.

"For a while, things settled a little. I was always with her up until she started pre-school, able to protect her from any kind of harm, and then I went through a stage of denial. I managed to convince myself that my husband wasn't a monster. We had a good year. But my fears returned when I found that my husband was spending long hours locked away in his office. I knew what he was up to in there, somewhere deep down, but I didn't want to believe it. And the worst thing about it was that I was so sure of what was going on, but I didn't have a shred of proof. I still don't. And I began to worry about what might happen if I wasn't around. Colton had began to snub me again, barely treating me as a human now that my body had no use to him. And as our daughter grew, I began to realize that someday, somehow, he would get rid of me. And then she would be alone with him, and I wouldn't be able to protect her. It made me sick to my stomach. And so I began to fantasize about killing him." She swallowed, guilt crossing her face. "I'm sorry… maybe I shouldn't admit that out loud. But I'm trying to be honest about what happened."

"It's okay. Thinking about killing someone isn't a crime. And we know you didn't do it, given that he's still alive and well," Brock assured her. "But I'm guessing you didn't stop completely at your fantasizing, did you?"

Terri shook her head. "No. I didn't. I was going to go through with it. I just didn't really have the means. But we had a particularly bad day. His parents had come over for dinner... and I began to get this feeling that his father wasn't right in the head either. He always had this strange vendetta against the priest at the local church... he always said what a weird kid he was, that he didn't believe he should be allowed to spend so much time with children. But I don't know... something told me that he only obsessed over it because he was like Colton. Inclined to... to... *want* young children. And I was beginning to spiral. I spent the whole day in a daze over it, tuning them all out. And when Colton went to the door to say goodbye to his parents... I went to the kitchen and found my sharpest knife. I was certain I was going to do it."

"What happened?"

Terri swallowed, her eyes filled with fear as she recalled the day.

"Our daughter was in bed... I faced off with him, but he overpowered me easily. He didn't try and talk me down. I think he knew of my suspicions. So he told me the horrible things he'd do to me if I tried to hurt him... and he reminded me that he could easily kill me. And then he'd be alone with our daughter. I didn't care much for my own life at that point... but I could never have left her alone with him. The thought was far too much to bear. And so I began to bargain with him. I pleaded. I told him that I could expose him for what he was... but that he had another choice. I told him that I'd take my daughter away. I'd leave and if he let me, it would buy my silence. I told him that he didn't want to hurt our baby girl... I told him that his sickness was his own to bear, but that to inflict it on our daughter... that would be a crime that could never be forgiven. And I got through to him. I knew I only had a narrow window to make my escape... but he had so many rules and regulations to make the separation work. He said he would provide for us, that I would stay within ten miles, that I would allow him to send letters to her. He said I'd have to cut ties with everyone else in the town, that I would have to virtually disappear... and he said he wouldn't allow me to date. He made me swear that no other man would be in her life. But I agreed. Of course I did. I didn't care about love… she was all that mattered to me. And so I agreed to everything. And I took her away in the middle of the night. There wasn't much else to do… I closed up my shop, deleted my contacts and started anew. But the threat of him being so close has had me living in fear for so long. And he still has so much control… he's ensured my silence, even though I haven't laid eyes on him in years now."

"I'm so sorry you've been through so much," Olivia said earnestly. Terri sniffed, wiping at her eyes desperately.

"You have no idea what it's like," Terri said, shaking her head. "Knowing that the man you fell in love with, the one you married… isn't right in the head. And in the end I kept my mouth shut because I was afraid for my daughter. He let me go, but he threatened to kill me if I ever exposed him, and I just couldn't risk that for my baby girl. If I die… she'll end up right back with him again. We never went through the courts and got a divorce, another one of the terms he made to keep control of me. So there's no reason he wouldn't get custody of her if something happened to me… and there is nothing worse than a child under the roof of a man like him. I couldn't stand the idea of her being preyed on by him, or hurt by him. A daughter shouldn't be afraid of her own father… I saved her before it was too late."

"Does she remember anything about him? Or did she ever say she was abused by him?" Brock asked. Terri shook her head.

"She was so young when we left… she can't even recall his face. But I made sure that he was never alone with her. I slept at her side and never let her out of my eyeline. But now that she's older, she wonders why she doesn't see him. She asks about him all the time. She wants to know where her daddy is… I have to tell her that he doesn't want to see her, because it's easier than explaining the truth. She's too young to understand what he could do to her, what his love for her meant…" Terri scrunched her eyes up, her emotions coming to a head. "She has all these fond ideas about him, fantasies that she's built because she has nothing else to work with, but she doesn't realize what he could do, even to his own child... and I won't put her through that. Even if it means her growing up without a father. Better to have no father than one like him."

"Did you ever think something might be happening to another child? Actively, I mean?" Olivia asked. "Did he ever..."

"No," Terri said firmly. "I knew his computer might contain... *explicit images*, but I never got the proof to use against him. He knew I was keeping a watchful eye on him... he rarely left the house without me or unless he was going to work. I don't think he could possibly have abused a child without me knowing. But I was so focused on our daughter... it never truly occurred to me. I have spent so many years trying to protect her. But when I saw the news about that young girl, Bethany... I had so many fears and doubts. And seeing him leading the investigation... I wondered about it, of course. I wish that I could give you more information, something solid... but I don't know what to do. I've been covering my own back, and my daughter's. The rest... the rest isn't my problem. I'm sorry if that makes me sound terrible... but I couldn't do a thing without risking my daughter anyway."

"You don't need to defend yourself right now. You've been living under threat for a long time," Olivia said gently. "But we're going to put all of this to an end, I promise. You and your daughter will be safe. Go now and collect her from school. Drive somewhere out of the way for a while and wait for us to contact you. We won't allow anything to happen to you."

"Thank you," Terri whispered, her eyes filled with unshed tears. "I'm so glad you came here. You're going to set us free."

"We'll do our best," Brock said. "But first, we need to put him away."

CHAPTER THIRTEEN

"**A**RE WE CERTAIN ABOUT THIS?" BROCK ASKED AS HE and Olivia got inside the car and prepared to drive to Colton Wright's home. "Because if we're not, we're making a pretty big accusation. And if we do, we'll blow any chances of being able to work with him again."

"All of the signs point in his direction," Olivia said firmly. "His disappearing wife and the threats he made, his father on the police force, Father Green's clues… the apple doesn't fall far from the tree, Brock. He's the only one that makes sense with all of the information we have."

"Have we considered that Father Green could be lying? The wife, too? That all this has been manipulated and planted by Adeline to mess with us? She lied last time. What if this is another misdirection?"

"To what end, Brock? If she misdirects us this much, there's no chance of us even following the trail she left us. You saw the state she was in on our last call."

"But still. I don't want to underestimate her. I'm just worried about this being another setup."

Olivia nodded. "We have to keep our eye out. But this isn't nothing—I mean, the news stories we found in the archive couldn't have been faked. And the girl has been missing for longer than we were even on this case. Why put us onto an active case and then manipulate us away from it?"

Brock stroked his chin thoughtfully. "You're right, of course. As usual. But we still don't have much solid evidence to go on. And if it is true, why does Father Green still live in this town where his abuser continues to live?"

"I guess it's better to live around the devil you know," Olivia pointed out, "And yes, there's a chance that Father Green is lying...but why would he? He was too afraid to even tell us who to look for. He said that he'd been threatened. I don't see any reason for him to lie about that."

"I don't know. We went in there because Tricia and Tom had their doubts about him. Is it possible that they were right to be wary of him?"

"Anything is possible, Brock. But we don't have the luxury of time here. We can either follow this lead to the end, or we can let it pass and hope something else comes up. But I have my suspicions about Wright too. He hasn't found a single lead since he began this investigation, has he? And when we showed up willing to help, he wanted to turn us away, even though we're experts. Don't you think that's suspicious?"

"I don't know what I think. You know how local cops can be when the FBI shows up. Maybe he just wants to be the one to take the glory when the case gets solved..."

"I don't think he ever wants this case to be solved, Brock. But I guess we're going to find his true intentions the moment we go to his home. The way he responds to our arrival is going to be very telling, I think. If he tries to turn us away, then I'm going to assume he has something to hide. Or else why would he do that?"

"I hope you're right about all of this."

Olivia frowned. "What's gotten into you? You're being very on the fence about this. Don't you think two witness statements are enough to point us in the right direction? Terri was clearly terrified of him. I don't imagine that both of them are lying. So why are you so uncertain about this?"

Brock sighed. "I guess... it's difficult to swallow. We're spread out, barely able to figure out if we're on the right track, chasing leads we have no way of properly investigating. Knowing that we're likely dealing with a dirty cop. A predator at that. Someone who is supposed to protect little girls, not harm them. It's hard enough to trust anyone in this line of work. Knowing we can't trust *anyone* is a pretty hard pill to swallow."

"Okay, first of all, that's not true, is it? We can trust each other a hundred percent. Do we really need more than that to get by? And secondly...there's one dirty cop for every hundred good ones, right? How many incredible cops have we worked with over the course of our careers? How many of them have helped us save children like Bethany from horrible fates? Don't lose faith. Just remember that in a world full of awful people, there are also incredible ones. The good outweighs the bad. That's why we do it, right? If there are dirty cops there, it's our job to put them away. To make sure they can't harm anyone ever again."

Brock sighed. "You make it sound so easy."

"I mean... we've taken down international human trafficking rings, Brock. Major drug lords, crazy cult leaders. If the worst we have to deal with is a small-town police department covering up each other's crimes, we can get to the bottom of it."

"But we're not dealing with that, are we? We're dealing with the Gamemaster. I just can't shake the feeling that her involvement in this means something."

"I know. But hey, even she has some good in her, right? She sent us here hoping we'd find Bethany alive. Even someone as evil as she is has a heart. That should tell us something about goodness in this world."

"I don't want to consider that she might be the good guy in this scenario," Brock said with a sigh. But then his expression softened, and he put his hand gently on Olivia's knee. "But you never lead us astray. I should have more faith. If you think this is the best lead we have, then who am I to argue?"

"Well, someone has to argue with me, play devil's advocate, right? Or else this whole thing would be far too simple."

Brock rolled his eyes, but he was smiling as he drove off, heading right for Wright's home. Olivia held her breath, drumming her fingers on the car door and praying that she'd gotten everything right. To her, it appeared that all signs were pointing in Colton Wright's direction, but if she was wrong, it would be a huge embarrassment for them, and the end of their involvement in the case. She desperately wanted to find the young girl alive and well, and she hoped that wasn't clouding her judgment.

But time wasn't on their side. If taking risks like this one would increase their chances of finding Bethany, then she was willing to give it a shot. The reward outweighed the risk in her mind. She'd take a lifetime of embarrassment to save the life of a single child. It was worth it. It had to be.

Colton's car was parked in front of his home when they arrived, and there was a light on in the living room. Brock parked out of sight of the house, taking a shaky breath. He checked his gun, glancing over at Olivia.

"You ready for this?"

"Yes."

"No last-minute doubts?"

Olivia wavered, but only for a second. She knew better than to ignore her instincts. Wright made sense as their culprit, and she wasn't going to back down because of last-minute nerves. She shook her head.

"No. It's him. I'm sure of it."

"Then let's end this. How do you want to play it?"

Olivia bit her lip, considering the question for a moment.

"Let's try and get a read on the room when we show up out of the blue. If he really did do something, then he's going to be nervous when we show up, especially if he's got something to hide in the house. If he shows even the slightest crack, take him down. I'll get inside and see what I can find."

Brock looked anxious at the suggestion. "We will get in so much trouble if we're wrong about this..."

"That's what he'll be relying on. Being a police officer has given him protection for far too long, and it has to end now. We might be the only people who can stop him. But we can't back down at the last moment. We'll find something to pin him."

"Okay," Brock said with a decisive nod. "I'll follow your lead."

Olivia took a steadying breath and then got out of the car. She knew that the second they confronted Wright, they were taking a big risk. He would be on high alert, and given the things they'd heard about him, he wasn't afraid to do anything to protect himself. It would be arrogant of him to hide Bethany in the house if he was truly the kidnapper, but then again, he'd been protected by his position for years. He had no reason to think they were on to him. Olivia hoped they were about to catch him completely off guard and save Bethany before anything went any further.

Olivia felt sick walking up to his home. The neighbors' homes were quiet, all of them unaware of what might be going on inside Wright's house. Olivia knocked at the door before she could talk herself out of it. She knew that they would have to be quick to find a way into the house, that Brock was going to have to hold Wright back to give her a shot at finding Bethany. And as the door opened, Olivia's breath was taken away at the height of the man, the bulk of him. He was a beast to contend with. But her face hardened. She wasn't the one who needed to fear him. A little girl was locked away somewhere, terrified of him.

She was going to save her.

"What are you doing here?" Wright asked gruffly, but was unable to keep the surprise from his tone. He clearly hadn't expected them to show up on his doorstep. Olivia kept eye contact with him, trying to keep her cool.

"Chief, we were hoping to come in and talk to you about the case. We were told you were off duty this morning, but I figured you'd want to hear the updates from us."

Colton's eyes searched Olivia's face, suspicion seemingly creasing his brow.

"Now isn't a good time…"

"Is that so?" Brock said coldly. "You got something else to be doing?"

"I'm exhausted from the case," Wright snapped. "I need time to recuperate."

"But we're telling you that we think we have a lead," Olivia said, a hint of a challenge in her voice. "And we need to come inside to talk about it."

The wording was enough to make Wright's expression waver. That was enough for Olivia. Wright had clearly clocked their meaning, knowing he was out of his depth with them. He launched for Olivia, but Brock was faster. He slammed into Wright, their bodies colliding with the wall as they fought one another. Olivia's heart skipped a beat. It was all happening too quickly, but if Wright was acting guilty, then that meant he had something to hide.

Or someone.

"Go, Olivia!" Brock cried out as Wright threw a punch at him, clocking the side of his cheek. Olivia was worried for her partner, but she was more concerned about the frightened, abused child that could be concealed in the house.

Olivia raced up the stairs and slammed the first door she came across open. There was nothing inside the bathroom. She continued while she heard Brock tussling with Wright downstairs. There was nothing in the small bedroom. But when she heard a muffled cry from down the hall, Olivia knew she had found what they'd been looking for.

Olivia opened the door to the master bedroom and found a young girl curled up on the bed. Her hands and feet were bound, and there was a gag in her mouth. Tears and snot stained her terrified face, and her eyes widened at the sight of Olivia's arrival. Olivia lost her breath for a moment.

"Bethany..."

She approached the scared child with caution, making soothing noises as she went to untie her. But Bethany didn't struggle as she untangled her from her bindings. And the moment she was free, she threw her arms around Olivia's neck, trembling in fear. Olivia held her close, stroking her hair gently and hushing her.

"It's okay, it's okay," she whispered. "Everything is going to be okay. You're safe now."

"Please don't let him tie me up again," Bethany cried in her ear. "I'm scared. I want my mommy and daddy."

"That man will never hurt you again. I'll keep you safe until you can be with your parents, I promise. You can go home very soon."

Olivia heard a cry from downstairs, and her heart jolted, but she knew it wasn't Brock. Clearly, he was winning the fight. Still gripping Bethany tight, Olivia rushed to the stairwell.

"I've got her!" Olivia cried out to Brock. She watched as he pressed his knee into Wright's spine to pin him down, handcuffing his hands behind his back breathlessly.

"Good," Brock wheezed. "I think it's about time we called for backup."

The hour that followed was a little strange and terrifying. When backup arrived, Olivia stayed with Bethany, listening to her testimony of events while Brock searched the rest of the house.

Bethany told the terrifying tale of the man she'd seen many times in the backyard, watching her through the window. And how one day, he'd broken into the house and put a gag on her before taking her away to his home. And now so much made sense—all along, the man in the garden had been none other than Police Chief Colton Wright. No wonder he'd dismissed Bethany's parents when they reported what they'd seen. The police were in on it all along.

Bethany told Olivia that Wright scared her, but that he had been trying to convince her that he was a good person. He'd told her many times that he wouldn't hurt her, that he would only love her and keep her safe. But the details that followed made Olivia want to cover her ears. Bethany claimed Wright had never touched her but that he had made her shower several times a day while he watched. Bethany had been aware of other things he was doing, but she had kept her eyes shut to block it all out. That felt like a small blessing to Olivia, though she knew those memories would scar Bethany for the rest of her life.

She continued to describe the experience to Olivia in a terrified whisper. He'd made her do other things she didn't really understand, things that made her feel scared even though he told her that she was safe with him. When he wasn't around, he would tie her up and close the curtains, leaving her on his bed. Then, at night, he would sleep beside her. She'd tried to figure out ways to escape, and she'd pleaded to go home, but nothing had come of her attempts. She was helpless and alone in her fear. Sometimes, she'd hear Wright listening to the news, talking about her disappearance. She knew there were people looking for her, so she didn't lose hope. She hadn't understood that Wright was the one supposedly leading the search for her, which Olivia took to be a blessing in disguise. At least, she had always thought someone was looking out for her.

Olivia listened intently to her tale, knowing that someone had to listen to the awful tale. And when it was over, she let Bethany crawl into her lap and cry while she waited for her parents to come. When Bethany's face was buried in her shoulder, Olivia allowed tears of her own to fall down her face.

And when Brock returned from searching Wright's office, he looked harrowed, too. Olivia knew exactly what he'd found in there—all of the inappropriate images that Terri had suspected him of storing on his computer. She dreaded to think exactly what was on there, and she felt glad that she hadn't had to see it herself. She hoped that Bethany had been shielded from it, too, among other things. Brock spoke in hushed whispers with the backup team while everything else unfolded around them.

It felt strange to watch the cop cars arrive to take Wright away. Police officers arresting other police officers was never going to be an ordinary situation, but there was no denying the things they had seen inside his house. Thankfully, the matter was in the hands of state police now, who would never be under Wright's thumb as the local police were.

Olivia had watched the reunion between Bethany and her parents with tears in her eyes, knowing that they had just saved a young girl from a terrible fate. Olivia dreaded to think what might have happened to her if they hadn't been called in to get involved in the case. It didn't bear thinking about.

The case was far from over, though. There was a whole web of lies to untangle with Wright, his father, and the other dirty cops at their station. The issues ran back further than Olivia cared to think about. But it wasn't for her to sort out. Their involvement in the case couldn't go any further. Not with Adeline's cruel games to contend with. Olivia hoped that the situation would be handled by the right people. Given the horror of the case, Olivia had no doubt that it would hit national news by the following day. At least then, they could be sure that Bethany's case got the attention it deserved. Perhaps even Father Green might get justice for the things Wright's father had put him through as well. It was awful to think that there might be other children in the town, abused by Wright's family for so long and left unprotected by the others on the force. At least Olivia could rest a little easier knowing that she had broken the chain.

The day was drawing to a close by the time Olivia felt comfortable leaving the case in the hands of the state police. She had spent a long while explaining to them all of the moving parts of the case—someone would need to do a deep dive into the corrupt police station, the issues possibly spanning for over twenty years, probably longer. But Olivia was determined that the awful issues would end with Wright. His daughter and Bethany would be safe from him now—he'd never see outside of a cell again. And Olivia was certain that a man like him would suffer as much as he deserved to in prison. Some got an easy ride on the inside of a jail, but if there was one guarantee in life, it was that the likes of Wright never had a moment of peace.

Olivia didn't mind that idea at all.

Olivia and Brock received a call from Adeline the moment they got back in the car to leave the scene. Olivia wondered how on earth she was keeping tabs on them, but she had no doubt that she had her ways. They answered the call wearily.

"Well done," Adeline said with a surprisingly warm smile. "You found her."

"Yeah," Olivia said tiredly. "It was messed up, as was what we found in Wright's home. But he won't get away with it now. He'll be in prison for life after what he did."

"I knew that I could rely on you. Call the first task a fluke... You guys are good at what you do," Adeline said, as if she were a proud mother talking to her children. Olivia raised an eyebrow.

"So you're glad we found her?" she asked. Adeline rolled her eyes.

"Of course I am. That's why I put you on this case in the first place. You just saved a young girl from being killed."

"I don't think he ever intended to kill her... but he did terrible things to that poor girl, I'm sure. Given the photographs we found... he intended to abuse her. I just hope he didn't get the chance to. Bethany is going to have a hard time recounting it all to the police and her parents. In fact, I don't think she'll ever be able to trust a cop again," Olivia said, barely able to talk aloud about the things they'd discovered.

"I'm sure she's traumatized by the things she saw and experienced in that creep's house... but at least she made it out alive. Sometimes that's the best thing we can hope for in life," Adeline said knowingly. Olivia wondered if she was speaking from experience. Was that what had messed Adeline up so much? Is that why she now went on murderous tirades, messing with people's lives, playing games to ruin people in ways they never imagined were possible?

Olivia frowned a little at the thought. But something else was bothering her too. Something about Adeline's choice to put them on the case in the first place. She knew she had to ask while she had the chance.

"I have a question, Adeline."

"That's Gamemaster to you. But sure. I guess you've earned that right."

"You said you've been following this case for a while. Since it started, really. And you've been watching all the press conferences and interviews..."

"That's right."

"And you... you suspected it was Wright all along, didn't you?"

Adeline shrugged, smiling as though she was pleased with herself. "I had a strong feeling about it. Something about him didn't sit right with me. I guess I've known a lot of weirdos in my time, and I saw him coming from a mile off. That's why I thought if I brought you guys in on the case, you would be able to sniff him out quickly and find Bethany. And now it's done and dusted, so problem solved, right?"

"Why didn't you say something sooner?" Brock said through gritted teeth. "About Wright? You could have saved Bethany days' worth of suffering."

Adeline looked a little hurt by the comment. "If I hadn't told you to get on the case, she likely would have died in that man's house or continued suffering at his hand. You're welcome, by the way."

"Forgive me if I don't feel very grateful to you," Brock snarled. "That may be true, but you could have just told us your suspicions. But no. You had to play your little games with us to mess us around. If you wanted her found, you could've told us to investigate him from the beginning, but you didn't. Because you care more about having fun with your dumb games than saving a child's life, so, stop pretending like you're some kind of saint for 'helping' us. I see right through you."

Adeline's smile was completely wiped from her face now. Olivia touched Brock's arm, warning him not to aggravate her. They both knew what she was capable of, and the last thing they needed was her finding some new way to try and torture them just because they made her mad.

"You're right," Adeline said after a few long moments. "I'm a monster. You got me. I don't know why you're so surprised, Brock. I've never pretended to be anything else. And I want you to suffer, so I'm just following through on what I told you I'd do all along. The child was just a detour. There, I said it. Are you satisfied now?"

"Completely," Brock said darkly. "Just as long as we're clear on everything. We know what you are. We're not fooled by one good deed. Or half a good deed, as you've just shown us."

"Sorry for trying to be helpful. It won't happen again," Adeline said. She sounded a little choked up, as though she was holding back tears, her throat tight. Olivia couldn't figure the Gamemaster out. Had she really expected them to be grateful for her contribution to the case? The more Olivia thought about it, the more cruel the Gamemaster's plan felt. She knew the whole time who the kidnapper likely was, but she kept quiet because she wanted to play games with their hearts. When they'd been put on the case, Olivia had felt as though the Gamemaster was trying to make up for her past. But now, the fog was clearing, and it was clearer than ever.

The Gamemaster only ever served herself.

Adeline seemed to have composed herself, scoffing at the pair of them.

"Well. I guess this one is finished. I'll send you the location for your next challenge. Don't worry. I have no intention of trying to save anyone in the next task," she said coldly. "This time around, things will be a little different. I'll give you forty-eight hours to get to the location and rest up as a reward for saving the child. Don't say I do nothing for you. But then you will be given only twenty-four hours to solve your next puzzle. It will take place in a single location, and you will find the captive inside the house I'm sending to you. That's all I'm telling you for now. I suppose I'll see you around."

She ended the call before Olivia or Brock could say anything. Brock scoffed.

"Why is she now acting like we've only just fallen out with her? Like she's mad at us for not hyping her up?" he asked, rolling his eyes. Olivia shook her head.

"We both know she's insane. She probably thought we were becoming friends."

"Well, far from it. Imagine being so crazy that you think you're a good person after everything she's done. She's delusional."

"She is. But she's also dangerous. So maybe next time, we should just keep our mouths shut. She said she was being lenient with us, but I don't trust her for a second. We should go straight to the location."

"Agreed. We can't allow anyone else to end up dead. And the sooner we solve this one, the closer we will be to the end of this whole thing. We're basically halfway now."

"Good," Olivia said. "Halfway to freedom."

CHAPTER FOURTEEN

O LIVIA AND BROCK WASTED NO TIME IN MAKING THEIR way to the location that the Gamemaster had provided to them. The mood was better in the car than it had been after the first task, and Olivia knew that they had done good, important work by finding Bethany. It was a small solace when they were being tugged here, there, and everywhere by such an evil woman, being made to play her stupid games.

But despite the Gamemaster's selfishness, Olivia still found herself surprised by her choice of task. She still felt as though Adeline Clarke had some shred of goodness inside her, otherwise why would she have made them try to save someone she didn't have plans to kill?

There was a vulnerability to the Gamemaster that they had yet to fully uncover. Brock didn't believe as much, but Olivia thought that if she was right, it would be their key to finally taking her down. If they could figure out what made her tick, then they would be one step closer to capturing her for good.

But the woman was exhausting. They'd been chasing her for so long now that it felt as if they would never be rid of her. And even after she'd been caught the first time, she'd managed to escape prison almost immediately. A villain like Adeline Clarke was the worst nightmare of an FBI agent like Olivia. She tested her limits and reminded her that not every case could be a complete success. Even after everything Olivia had achieved in her career, someone like Adeline made her feel like she wasn't capable of anything at all. She hated that feeling. The one thing she had always been able to rely on was her own skills and her capabilities at work. Even when everything else was falling apart, those skills remained a constant. But it was impossible to feel confident in herself when she'd become used to failing at every turn, outsmarted by one of the few people capable of taking her down a few notches.

But that didn't mean she planned to give in. Olivia dug her nails into her palms for the entire journey, staying alert, trying to guess what they might be about to face. The drive was long, and it took them up past Baltimore, past Philadelphia, along the coastline, and up into upstate New York. At some point, she dozed off for a while, and when she woke up again, the car was slowing down, and a huge mansion was coming into view. Olivia's eyes widened as she took in the place. She'd seen a lot of grand houses in her life, and her cases often had her mingling with rich folk, but this was something else.

"Is this where the Gamemaster wanted us to go?" she asked Brock in disbelief. He checked the coordinates they'd been given.

"Looks like it. There's nothing much else around here anyway, so this must be it. She did say we'd be going to a house…"

"A house, yes, but not a palace."

"It is pretty impressive," Brock said, admiring the huge gothic structure with interest. "I wonder why the Gamemaster picked this place, though."

"Who knows? Maybe she has a vendetta against whichever rich recluse lives inside there. I wouldn't be surprised if this task was personal... to single in on one house and to give us a shorter time limit as a result... this one feels a little different again. I feel like the deeper into these tasks we get, the more we are learning about Adeline."

"I've learned enough about that woman to last me three lifetimes," Brock grumbled. "I don't care what's going on in there. I just want to get it over and done with so that we can move on with our lives. But something tells me it won't be that simple... how are we even going to get inside? That gate is an obstacle in itself."

Olivia glanced at the huge metal gate that guarded the house. Brock was right—they needed to tackle that before they even thought about searching for the missing person. But as though on cue, the Gamemaster began to call them. Brock sighed and picked up the call. The Gamemaster's mood had shifted back to cheerful and cheeky, a far cry from the end of their last call. She grinned at them.

"I see you've made it to the house. Or should I say... home sweet home. Yes, that's right. This is my house. Or one of them. This is where I grew up."

Olivia shot a knowing glance at Brock. She *knew* there was something personal about this task, something that made this close to home for Adeline. She just hadn't realized just how literal that would be.

"Sorry I can't be there to give you a tour, but I guess I'm a little busy these days," Adeline teased them. "But let me run over the rules with you again before I open up the gates. You'll have twenty-four hours to find someone inside the house. Who, I hear you ask? Well, it's someone very special to me. A relative of mine, in fact."

103

Olivia blinked in horror. "What?"

Adeline smiled. "That caught you off guard, didn't it? Well, allow me to explain to you. Home isn't necessarily where the heart is. I have some unresolved issues to sort through, and I figured you'd be able to help me out. So a member of my family is hidden somewhere inside the house. Their life is in your hands. Save them, or don't. I don't care either way. But be quick about it! The clock will start ticking the moment I open the gates for you."

"Why would you do this?" Brock asked. "Your own family... and we know what happened to your parents. You can't have that much family left. Why would you want to try and destroy your family even more?"

Adeline rolled her eyes with a short laugh. "Stop trying to attach meaning to everything, Brock! Let's just call me crazy and move on, shall we? Sometimes there isn't a reason. Sometimes people do things just for the hell of it. Okay? Now, if you're done with all of your boring questions, I'll open up the gates. God, talking to you guys is so annoying sometimes."

Adeline ended the call before Brock could respond and he let out an irritated grunt. Olivia was more than happy to just get on with things. She was sure now that whatever lay inside the house—and who—would tell them a lot more about the person they were trying so hard to chase down. Adeline had laid herself bare by inviting them into her childhood home, whether she was aware she was doing it or not. Now, Olivia planned to use that to her advantage.

The gate cranked open for them, and Brock drove them inside the perimeter, muttering to himself irritably. Olivia put a gentle hand on his arm.

"Don't let her get to you. We've got a job to do."

"I know. I just need my two minutes of grumpiness. It gets it out of my system. God, she knows how to wind me up."

"And she knows it," Olivia reminded him. "She's just trying to get to you so that you'll take your eye off the ball."

"I won't let that happen. But twenty-four hours to find a person in one house? How hard can it be?"

Olivia had secretly been wondering the same. Sure, the house was huge, but they could likely walk around the whole place within a few hours at most. It seemed like there must have been a catch, as there was so often with the Gamemaster. Olivia's mind began to mull over a thousand possibilities—secret hiding places, booby traps, assassins waiting in the dark to strike them down. After all, they'd been warned already that they were being hunted down. But Olivia knew the only way to find out what they were facing was to go inside and face it head-on.

The door to the mansion opened without any resistance. The place had been waiting for their arrival. Olivia was amazed by the beauty of the place—the tall ceilings, the gorgeous decor, and the magnificent grandeur of it all. But there was a darkness to the place that she couldn't quite put her finger on. It seemed like the place had been empty for a long time, frozen in time from long ago. Olivia's nose tickled, and she realized that everything in the place was covered in a thick layer of dust.

And then there was the silence. The chilling, complete silence. Like nothing had ever lived or breathed in the house. Was that how their Gamemaster had felt growing up in this place? Like there was never enough air, even in a house so vast? Like there was no life or love breathed into the place, no matter how far the walls stretched and the ceilings loomed?

"This place is…something," Brock said quietly, as though trying not to wake the house. Olivia swallowed, a chill running down her spine. She looked around her, wondering where on earth to begin. There were so many corridors leading off the entrance hall, plus two mirrored staircases leading up to the other floors. It was intimidating, especially when they were losing time the longer they stood there.

"I think we need to be tactical to start out with," Olivia said. "I think we need to try and find Adeline's childhood bedroom."

"And I suppose you think there will be clues in there? Olivia, this house looks like it hasn't had a single visitor for a decade. I doubt Adeline has planted anything to help us out, and I don't think she even planned for this weird challenge as a child. What can we possibly find in her bedroom that will help us now?"

"Who knows? But I think the key is there. Adeline is clearly a troubled woman. That likely started in childhood. As far as we know, she had very absent parents, so what did that do to her? What else can we learn from this place? I think there must be something of her old self left behind here. I'm not saying she wanted us to find it… but if we can get inside her head from when she was a child, maybe we can unlock information about what she's thinking as an adult. Maybe we can even figure out who the relative is and why she might be tempted to do something awful to them. I'm not crazy for thinking that, right?"

Brock sighed. "No. Not at all, actually. I'm just being a pessimist, I guess. I need to get in the zone."

"Get there fast," Olivia said, making her way toward the staircase. "Twenty-four hours isn't as long as it seems."

CHAPTER FIFTEEN

"**H**OW ARE WE EVEN SUPPOSED TO FIND HER BEDROOM? There must be a thousand rooms up here," Brock said as he followed Olivia down the long corridor of the first floor. She rolled her eyes to herself.

"Perhaps a slight exaggeration, Brock."

"Okay, yeah, but I'm still wondering how best to identify it. It's like you said. We're against the clock. What are we looking out for?"

"Well, I don't know, to be honest. I don't even know how old she was when she was living in this house. She's still young now, so it can't have been that long ago that she was here. But we know that her parents traveled a lot for work. They probably didn't make much time for her here… they probably didn't care much about giving her a childhood bedroom. Maybe it won't be obvious at all that her room once belonged to a child."

"Great. Well, that's helpful, then."

"About as helpful as your attitude, Brock. Get your head in the game. It's not helping to be negative."

"Sorry. Noted."

They explored the first-floor corridor thoroughly. Olivia was even shocked by how far the rooms seemed to span, each of them so big on the inside that it was hard to furnish them enough to make them seem worth their size. The furniture was elegant and old-fashioned, matching with the style of the house. There were some modern amenities, including huge televisions, but the four-poster beds and old paintings kept the place from feeling like it was from the twenty-first century.

And even as they explored bedroom after bedroom, none of them gave much indication that they had belonged to Adeline. In fact, the whole house seemed completely unsuited to a young person. There were no toys or items that might suggest that they encouraged her to have hobbies. With the old-fashioned decor, Olivia was half expecting to stumble across old grand pianos and easels to paint on, something at least to train the mind of someone as creative as the Gamemaster had proved to be. But there was little at all, and Olivia was beginning to wonder whether they were being messed with yet again. Had Adeline Clarke ever lived in the house at all?

But when they reached the end of the first-floor corridor, feeling confused and disorientated, Olivia noticed that the final room had a lock on it. Frowning, Olivia walked over to the door and took the padlock in her hand, giving it a rattle. It was definitely locked.

"Why would they padlock the door?" she mused out loud. There was nothing as intriguing to a detective as a locked room, and Olivia knew that they needed to get inside. But without a key, it would be a case of breaking down the door.

"I can see the cogs turning in your head, but don't bother," Brock said, waggling a dusty key at Olivia. "It was on the windowsill. I guess whoever put the lock on there wasn't so bothered about keeping someone out of there ... but more keeping something or something *inside.*"

"You don't think ... you don't think this is Adeline's bedroom, do you? That her parents locked her inside to keep her there?"

"I don't know. They certainly weren't a traditional family... but to lock a child in a room in a house this big seems very harsh. What's the point of all this space if it's not allowed to be used?"

"True, but we know Adeline is a troublemaker. Maybe it was a precaution, or even a necessity, to stop her from running wild. I mean, we know her now as a problem, but maybe that started in this house. Maybe her parents put the lock on the door for their own sanity."

"But ... but we're not looking for her parents, are we? They're already dead, and we know they weren't around much in Adeline's childhood. They can't have kept her locked in her room every time they went away, she'd starve to death. So maybe the relative that's hidden in the house, the one we're supposed to find... maybe they were the one who kept Adeline locked up."

"I never thought I would say it, but if that's the case, then I feel sorry for Adeline. What an awful thing to be put through. And by your own family, too."

"Don't humanize her," Brock warned Olivia, slotting the key inside the lock. "I think that's the worst mistake we can possibly make when she's torturing us this way."

Olivia nodded in understanding, but she didn't fully agree. As much as she wanted to turn her back on Adeline completely and treat her like any other criminal, she was starting to feel like she knew her far too well to ignore the way she'd turned out. Young Adeline had clearly been lonely, desperate to play games with a family who didn't make time for her, far too intelligent for her own good. Did she ever stand a chance when she started out her life in such a strange and lonely way?

As the door to the room opened, Olivia knew that they were right—this was Adeline's bedroom at one time. The room wasn't particularly personal, with another identical four-poster bed and the same ancient paintings on the walls, but there was a desk in there with an old laptop sitting on it, plus a few other items. There was no sign of any toys in the room, or posters, or anything that Adeline might have chosen for herself. Everything seemed to be functional and practical. Olivia had always thought growing up in a mansion would mean that a child was left wanting for nothing. But Olivia could now picture young Adeline holing up alone in the dark room, with only her laptop to keep her entertained and no one to talk to. Was it any wonder that Adeline had created the Gamemaster persona for herself, resorting to playing cruel tricks on other people to keep herself entertained?

"She must've spent so much time in here alone," Olivia said, trailing her finger along a dusty old chest of drawers. She opened it and found a few old sets of clothes in there, but nothing looked like they belonged to a rich child growing up in a house full of grandeur. Like someone had just picked any old thing in her size and given it to her to wear. The clothes had no color, no personality, nothing. "Maybe she didn't ever really learn how to socialize… did she ever mention being homeschooled?"

"Does it matter?"

"Of course it matters. Homeschooling would have meant that she was completely devoid of interaction with other kids her age. Imagine if she never really left this room… never got to speak to her peers, never got to learn and play and make mistakes with other kids. That would've been damaging in itself. But with no freedom to even leave her bedroom… it's no wonder she's so messed up now." Olivia paused, turning to Brock. "I don't think she brought us here just to play this game and to find her relative. I think she wants us to know the story of her. This is her last big hurrah, or so she says. I think this is her way of trying to show the world what made her the way she is now. She's spent all this time creating a persona for herself as the Gamemaster. She's used to being the center of attention now, but she spent so many years in the dark, unperceived. This is her way of communicating with us without saying a word."

"And she expects us to feel sorry for her?"

"Probably. She's a narcissist. She's obsessed with herself. Which makes total sense, if you think about a life spent in this room with no one else. It's hard to imagine that anyone outside of your life matters when you've never even been given the chance to know anyone outside of these four walls. She was brought up to not care about anyone else."

"Well, we knew that much already."

Olivia moved over to the laptop on the desk. "Imagine letting the internet raise you, Brock. That was potentially her only communication with the outside world. If she was left on there unmonitored…I can only imagine the things she came across. That's enough to bring the darkness out of anyone. And then her obsession came with her own games channel…by the time she was old enough to get into it, to use her parents' money to create her own mini-empire…I guess she'd already formed her personality. But I think she's changing."

"How so?"

"The island was her first attempt at something truly cruel. Before then, she was just like any other vlogger, really. She would set those games and puzzles for people, but it never was anything on this scale. Then she decided to do something that truly set her apart, but it obviously got out of hand and turned out to be absolutely horrendous. And yes, she seemed to get a taste for it for a while. All that power… killing people—or watching us all killing ourselves on the island—that appealed to her at first, clearly. And then she spent many months after her escape setting all of this up. But these little looks into her personality tell us so much. Making us save a young girl from a horrible fate, having us search for a relative who hurt her in her own house…"

"And what about the random man who she killed in his own store and then burned his corpse? Olivia, this is craziness. Acting

ELLE GRAY | K.S. GRAY

like she's some kind of rational human who has just messed up a few times. She murdered people for entertainment. Have you forgotten how she made Yara kill Jonathan? Have you forgotten how she gatecrashed your cousin's funeral to send us on a wild goose chase?"

Olivia sighed. "No, Brock, of course not. I can never forget the ways she has tortured us. But this is how we understand her. She *wants* us to understand her, whether consciously or not. She's drawing our eyes back to her at every turn. She's reminding us what she's capable of, but she's also trying to teach us why she does the things she does. I'm not saying that it excuses any of it. It doesn't at all. But the more we know, the better we can understand what her next move will be. Do you see what I'm saying?"

Brock pinched the bridge of his nose, looking pained.

"I do. I understand. I'm sorry, I'm not trying to be difficult. She just affects me in a way no one else does. She's taken so much from us both, put us through so much… I don't want to act like this could be just anyone turning out the way she has. I don't want to think that she's just some product of her environment. I want to hate her. I *do* hate her. And your fascination with her… it's hard to swallow."

Olivia's expression softened. "I'm sorry… I guess I'm just not used to being focused on one person for so long in our work. We've been chasing her for so long, and she's been chasing us right back. She's made an impression on me. And I guess I just find myself curious about her. This job has always been fascinating, but it's not often that we study someone so complex. She's got my attention."

Brock chewed his lip. "I know. It's good to be curious about this line of work. That's what makes you so good at it. You always see things that others would likely miss. But this has just been one long, continuous nightmare. I want it to be over."

"Me too, trust me. I don't think I've rested well since this whole thing began. And I don't want to be caught up in it any longer than we have to. But until it's over… I'm just getting inside her head. Keeping myself alert for clues. Especially because you've been so...so..."

"Angry? Frustrated? Yeah, I have, you're right," Brock said, his voice a little terse. "We just have different approaches on this one, I suppose. I don't want to overlook everything she's capable of."

"I promise, we won't. I know who she is. I just want to know a bit more. I don't see the harm in that."

Brock suppressed a sigh. "Well, it might come back to bite us, but we can't just stand around pulling guesses out of thin air to find this relative. You're right. We have to dig deep. Do you think we can get that old laptop working?"

"I think we should definitely try. I think this room will have everything we're looking for," Olivia said firmly. She knew Brock had his doubts about what the room could tell them, but Olivia was sure that the key to figuring out which relative they were trying to find would be in the room. It might even tell them where they would be hidden and how to get to them.

However, one thing Olivia hadn't considered was how to hack into the computer of a former teenage genius who had no equipment to help them crack it. She tried a few times to work out the password but to no avail. She swore quietly under her breath. She had learned something about their Gamemaster after all—she was too smart for them, even as a teenager.

But it was Brock who hit the motherlode. He upturned a dusty pillow and pulled something out from underneath it, holding it up triumphantly.

"Can't go wrong with a diary in an investigation," Brock said, passing it over to Olivia. She took a look at the leather-bound book. The pages were fluffed up and thick, extra pages stuck into the back of it with crude scotch-taping skills. It was definitely well-used, and Olivia wondered if Adeline had found solace in noting her thoughts down. After all, it appeared there wasn't really anyone around to listen to her.

"You keep looking. Maybe try the laptop again. I'll take a look," Olivia said, sitting on the bed and wrinkling her nose as a powder puff of dust rose from the sheets. Coughing a little, she opened up the first few pages of the diary.

Dear Diary,

It's my birthday today. Mom and Dad couldn't make it back to celebrate with me—apparently they've got some super important meetings today—but they did get me this diary, so that's cool, I guess. I asked them if I could travel with them soon… they said they'd let me once I'm old enough. But I've just turned thirteen and, apparently, that still isn't old enough. So I've got another year to kill in his dumb old house with Aunt Teresa.

Aunt Teresa… could this be the relative they were supposed to be searching for? Olivia felt pretty confident that she must be an important character in Adeline's tale if she was supposedly the one keeping an eye on her while her parents weren't around. And it didn't seem like Adeline appreciated her presence much. Olivia flicked a few pages.

Dear Diary,

I'm going crazy in this stupid house. I can't remember the last time Aunt Teresa let me go outside. She's so weird. She told me that she's afraid of going outside, but how does that make any sense? Does she really expect to just stay in this house forever? Maybe. It's bad enough that I have to stay at home to learn, but I never see anyone other than her these days. My parents haven't been for a visit in forever. Visit? Hah! It's their house, and they already feel like strangers here. What a joke.

I wouldn't mind, but I have to live by all of Aunt Teresa's rules. She makes me eat all the stuff she likes, and we do what she says, and she makes me sit and watch her shows with her. I take it back. I'd rather never see anyone again than spend another second with Aunt Teresa.

Olivia wavered for a moment over the next few pages. It sounded as though Adeline's aunt was a bit strange and had some unusual quirks, but she didn't seem to be too terrible yet. But Olivia was sure there was more to the story than Adeline just being irritated by her family. When had the lock appeared on her door? When had the house become a complete prison instead of her home? Olivia flicked forward a little, wanting to know how the story progressed.

Dear Diary,

Not much to report. There never is. The days are all the same in this house. I get up in the morning, and Aunt Teresa gives me my lessons. Then we take a walk from the top floor to the basement, then back up and down once more. She says it's good for me to get my exercise, and it takes forever, but I don't understand why I can't just walk around the grounds. I've forgotten what fresh air is like, to be honest. Sometimes I try to crack the window open a little further and stick my head out, but Aunt Teresa did something to them to make them stick after a certain point.

After the walk, Aunt Teresa says we have to hone our minds so we play chess over and over until I want to throw a rook at her stupid head. Then there's Chinese checkers as a palate cleanser, as she calls it, and then she times me while I complete Sudoku puzzles for a while. I used to enjoy the games, sort of, but now it's repetitive and they're too easy and it just makes me angry with her to the point where I want to scream. She yells at me every time I talk back, though, so it just isn't worth it. I do as I'm told so that she doesn't lash out at me like she did the time when she struck me with her old umbrella. I had a welt on my back that wouldn't go away for weeks.

When Aunt Teresa decides it's time to watch her mind-rotting shows, I go back to my room and hit the internet. I talk to people in chat rooms, but no one really gets me. All these old guys try and hit on me, or kids are just talking about school, and I have nothing in common with them. It just makes me feel depressed. So when I get fed up with that, I'll sometimes make up all these scenarios in my head of what I will do when I'm allowed out of this dump. Mom and Dad tell me that when they die I'll be super rich because they'll give all of their money to me. I'm going to spend it on getting out of here and doing something with my life. I'm too smart to be trapped in an old house rotting away. Someday, I'll show the world what I'm made of.

Olivia felt her stomach twist. It was becoming clear to her exactly how Adeline had evolved. She had been right. Her upbringing had changed her. But there still seemed to be something missing from the tale. Some kind of trigger point that would make it all come together and make sense. As Olivia flicked forward through the entries, the handwriting became more and more scribbled, getting bigger as though young Adeline was screaming out her thoughts, desperate to be heard. But Olivia suspected no one had seen her words until she had right at that second.

Dear Diary,

I'm so alone in all of this. I can't tell anyone about what is happening to me. I don't think anyone would believe me anyway. My friends online think I'm so lucky because I live in such a big, beautiful old house. But this house has its ghosts, and someday, if Aunt Teresa has her way, maybe I'll be one of them.

She's been hitting me a lot lately. Everything I do seems to upset her. Either I'm not understanding work fast enough, or not completing our walk in record time, or I'm being lousy at puzzles, but I'm so tired. I can't sleep because my back hurts where she hits me with the metal umbrella. She tells me to stop being a baby every time she hits me, saying it doesn't hurt, but it does. I know I'm not being a baby. My back is black with bruises, and it only slows me down more. I'm on edge trying to keep up with her demands, but I never manage to do it.

And now, after she hits me, she locks me inside my room. Sometimes for a few days at a time. She doesn't bring me food or water, so I've started rationing things, hiding them in my pocket just in case she does it again. I've been going to the bathroom in the corner of the room. Like an animal. It's disgusting. And then Aunt Teresa gets mad again and wants to hit me more.

I tried to open the window and get out again, but it's too far to fall down even if I did manage to get it open. It would kill me.

Maybe that wouldn't be so bad. It would be quicker than letting Aunt Teresa kill me. I've started making a mark in the back of the book every time she hits me. It's getting full.

I don't know how much more of this I can take.

Olivia swallowed. This was exactly the kind of thing she had been looking for. She pictured that Adeline might have had a neglectful childhood, but nothing like this. Nothing so dark and bleak. She had truly suffered under her aunt's hand, in the very room where they were sitting. Olivia looked up from the diary, her head pounding. Brock sat down beside her.

"Did you find anything?"

"I think we're looking for her aunt," Olivia said solemnly. "She was brought up by her… but she was abusive. It seemed like she had some kind of obsessive need to keep them both inside the house, and it got worse and worse. She started hitting Adeline and locking her in her bedroom. It was really bad, Brock. Here, take a look."

Brock flicked through some of the pages. When he got to the end, Olivia spotted something she hadn't seen before.

There were pages and pages marked with tallies. Olivia realized what it was for. It was the amount of times her auntie had hit her. The tallies went on for pages and pages, seemingly endless. Olivia's heart squeezed in her chest. She didn't feel as sorry for Adeline as she was now—she had made her choices in life.

But she mourned the child who had suffered so much. That child had been beaten to death by someone who was supposed to love her. And from her corpse, the Gamemaster had been born. So many tragic stories started that way. Olivia was all too familiar with those types of tales. But hearing Adeline's made her seem more human than she ever had before.

"Don't do it to yourself," Brock warned her again. "Remember who we are dealing with."

"I know. It's nearly impossible to forget. But this is horrible, Brock. Don't you think her inviting us here was some kind of messed-up call for help? A final last-ditch attempt to be heard because no one paid attention when she was a child who needed saving?"

"That might be true. But she's no damsel in distress," Brock said, slamming the diary shut. "Don't forget, she plays games better than anyone. And now she's in your mind. Just like she wanted, probably, so consider this. Is she playing the long game? Has she *always* been playing the long game? Don't trust her for a second." Brock took a deep breath. "That's how we will wind up dead."

CHAPTER SIXTEEN

L
EAVING ADELINE'S BEDROOM, OLIVIA AND BROCK WERE
faced with the true task of the day—finding Aunt Teresa.
At least, Olivia assumed that was who they were looking
for. After everything she had read in the diary, it made sense
that Adeline would want to punish the person who wronged
her so much in her childhood. If Olivia were in her shoes, she
imagined that would be her biggest target in life. Adeline had
certainly revealed herself as a vengeful woman, and Olivia
thought that the diary clearly laid out exactly why she would
want Aunt Teresa to suffer. But they had a chance to save her
life if they could only figure out where she was. Even a woman
as cruel as Aunt Teresa didn't deserve to be murdered.

Now, it was just a matter of finding her in the house. Olivia knew that they had twenty-four hours ahead of them for the task—twenty-two if they counted exploring the first floor and Adeline's bedroom—but it all seemed a little too easy. There was no chance that they were going to need all of the time they had been given. There was another floor above the one they'd already looked through, and then the ground floor and the basement. Even if they spent a few hours searching each floor and then possibly a few more looking through the grounds, they would easily cover the ground within the time limit. That made the whole thing feel a little too good to be true. And when it came to the Gamemaster, that often meant something more sinister.

Olivia didn't want to think that way. It meant that she was being pessimistic, and the Gamemaster had implied that she wanted to play a fairer game now. She had, after all, allowed them to save a little girl from a terrible fate, and she seemed to be growing fonder of Olivia and Brock in her own strange way. Perhaps she really was going easier on them, wanting to see them succeed rather than crashing and burning. After reading her diary, Olivia felt she could assume something better of the Gamemaster by now. She was more complex than Olivia had ever imagined. Her past had built her into a monster, but Olivia was sure there could be some redemption for Adeline. Or at least, she could stop doing such terrible things if only she could find the will to be better.

But there was a nagging feeling in the back of Olivia's mind, telling her everything couldn't be as it seemed. It couldn't be as simple as searching the vast house and finding a woman before the time ran out. She felt sure that there had to be some obstacles in the way or something to stop them from achieving the task. After all, this was supposed to be a game, and they had yet to truly figure out the rules. That put Olivia on edge more than anything, and she found herself taking every step with extra caution.

But nothing stood in their way. They searched the top floor and the ground floor without finding anything but more dusty furniture that had been long abandoned. Then, desperate for a reason to spend a little time outdoors where dust wouldn't fill their lungs, they searched the grounds, but the overgrown grass revealed nothing but unkempt weeds.

Olivia and Brock returned to the house, the bottom of their pants damp from the grass. They were tired and feeling a little frustrated by their lack of progress. They only had the basement to search now, and if they didn't find Aunt Teresa then they were indeed being tricked.

"Are we missing something here?" Olivia asked. "Maybe we need to read more of the diary… what about Adeline's routine with her Aunt? She talked about having to walk the house from top to bottom. Do you think it'll reveal something if we do that? Or maybe there's a clue in the puzzles and games her aunt made her play…"

"Maybe. But on the other hand, we could just be overthinking this. We've checked every nook and cranny of this place so far. Sure, we've found a few hidden rooms behind sliding bookcases, but even those were as empty and dusty as the others. The only place left to go is the basement. But given that basements are usually creepy and gross, we should probably have thought to check there first," Brock pointed out. Olivia chewed her lip.

"I know. Maybe you're right. But don't you feel like something is off? Like we're missing something? I just feel like she's made this far too simple. If Aunt Teresa really is down there, then we've solved this with plenty of time to spare… and the Gamemaster knows how to plan the game of a lifetime. There's got to be some kind of twist."

"Maybe she's expecting us to think there's a twist, and the real twist is there's no twist. For all we know, there's no one here. She probably just wants to see us scrabbling around trying to solve this thing while exploring her childhood home. She probably loves the idea of us rooting around in the psyche of her teenage self. It seems like the sort of thing she'd take weird pleasure in. We should just get down to the basement and see what's there. If we don't find anything, then I guess we can recheck the house. Either way, there's sixteen hours left to play with. No need to panic just yet, right?" He smiled, but it wasn't very encouraging.

Olivia sighed. The exhaustion was getting to her now. She was starting to wish they'd taken the opportunity for a break between the tasks just to catch their breath. They could both benefit from a good night's sleep and maybe then this whole mess would make more sense to her. But Olivia told herself that she could sleep once they found Aunt Teresa. She was a bad person if everything in the diary was to be believed, but that didn't mean Olivia was willing to stop and just let her die. They had a job to do, and they couldn't give up now. Not when they were likely so close to the truth.

And possibly one step closer to understanding the Gamemaster herself.

"I didn't see a way into the basement, did you?" Brock asked, interrupting her thoughts.

"I think there was a door to it through the kitchen, at the back of the house. We didn't take a look in there, did we? I guess it used to be used for food storage or something."

"Well, it's worth a look. Shame we have to walk through the rest of this creepy house to get there…"

Olivia didn't mind the idea of looking through the house a second time. With every step she took through the musty halls, she felt more like she was walking in Adeline's shoes. As they walked through the dining hall, she imagined a young girl sitting alone for dinner while her parents were away, wishing that they might return and pay some attention to her. In the living room, she imagined Adeline staring blankly at the TV, forced to watch Aunt Teresa's trashy shows while feeling wholly misunderstood and alone. There was a games room where she could picture the young woman winning at chess over and over, her brilliant mind blossoming but also twisting into something cruel as she became more bitter and jaded.

By the time Olivia and Brock made it to the kitchen, Olivia had a clear picture of who Adeline was, who she had become, and what her future looked like. It was her job to build a profile of a killer and to figure them out, but she'd never spent quite as long in the mind of the others as she had with Adeline Clarke. She was the one who kept returning to her, no matter how much she wished to be rid of her.

And there was one thing Olivia was sure about when it came to the Gamemaster. Nothing would ever be enough for her after such a deprived childhood. She would always be chasing a way to fill the hole in her heart, creating games and pain and cruel brilliance just to give herself some kind of purpose. She had never learned how to love, and all of that energy had instead gone into learning evil. It made Olivia sad to think about it. Adeline was a monster, but she hadn't been born that way.

She had been forged.

"Looks like this is it," Brock said, gesturing to the basement door. "Do you think the place is rigged or something? We should probably watch our step."

"We'll be cautious. Maybe that's the twist we've been waiting for. I'd be surprised if it was as simple as finding her."

"Well, there's only one way to find out. I guess we're about to find Aunt Teresa."

"I hope she's okay. Though it's going to be hard to explain to the police how the hell we found her. Or why we're here in the first place." Olivia said.

"We'll cross that bridge when we get to it. We might be getting ahead of ourselves. She might not even be here."

Brock turned the handle of the door. It gave way without any protest. But an awful smell wafted up from the basement. as the door opened Brock gagged and stepped back, covering his nose. His eyes met Olivia's.

"What does that smell like to you?"

"A dead person," Olivia whispered. She took the lead, grabbing her phone and turning on the flashlight. Slowly, the pair of them descended into the dark, dank room. She checked the floor as she walked, but she saw no sign of traps or obstacles. Olivia pulled her shirt up over her mouth, trying not to breathe in the terrible stench. She shone the light into the room, afraid of what she was about to see.

It was there she saw the chair.

Sitting on it was a woman.

Or what used to be a woman.

Now, all that was left was a rotting corpse with a knife sticking out of its back.

CHAPTER SEVENTEEN

"WHAT THE HELL?" BROCK MURMURED, approaching the dead woman in the chair, his hand still covering his mouth. The smell was terrible, and Olivia knew that there was no chance this woman was still alive when they had been put on the case. The stench alone indicated that her death had occurred some time ago. Days or even weeks, maybe. When she got closer, the smell intensified, and it became even clearer that the woman had been there for a while. Her face had begun to melt away from her bones, and they would likely have a hell of a time trying to identify the body. There were few indicators that the person was even a woman, other than the longer hair clinging to her scalp.

"Is it some kind of trick?" Olivia wondered out loud. "Like a decoy body? Maybe this isn't the relative we're supposed to be looking for. Maybe this is just a sick joke from the Gamemaster to have us give up too early…"

"I don't know… I'll search the body," Brock said. He untied the woman's corpse and pulled on a pair of gloves before laying her down on the floor. Olivia winced at just how decomposed the body was. Flies buzzed around the basement. They rarely saw a body in such a gruesome state, and it was harder to stomach than usual. But they still needed to know who the woman was and whether this was a part of the task the Gamemaster had set out for them.

Brock managed to pull a wallet out of the woman's jeans and he produced a driver's license from inside it. He sighed.

"It's her. Teresa Marsh. That must be her mother's sister."

Olivia closed her eyes. So it had been another stupid game for them to get caught up in. The Gamemaster had clearly killed Aunt Teresa days—maybe even weeks—earlier and just left her there for them to find. After everything they'd read in the diary, Olivia knew she shouldn't be surprised. If there was one person that Adeline should've been seeking revenge on, then it should be the dead woman in front of them. But Olivia's compassion for Adeline was fading fast. She hadn't even given them a chance to save her. That wasn't part of the deal. The tasks they were given were hard, but they shouldn't be impossible. If they weren't even given the opportunity to save their victims, then what was the point in it all? Other than to riddle them with guilt, perhaps? Maybe that was enough of a prize for the Gamemaster. Maybe she was somewhere now, laughing to herself at how ridiculous two FBI agents were being made to look, chasing smoke they'd never catch up with.

But that was the way of the Gamemaster. She had never played by the rules, not even by the ones she set out herself.

She'd obviously done this for a reason—either to torture them with the impossibility of their tasks, or simply to humiliate her aunt with an undignified death, never given the opportunity for redemption. Olivia supposed that Adeline had never been given an option either. Perhaps the payback was justified in Adeline's mind. Olivia was simply lucky enough not to understand how that must feel.

"What are we supposed to do now?" Brock asked. "We can't just leave her here."

"I suppose we should call the police. Our fingerprints are going to be all over this place," Olivia murmured. "And we need to report the dead body. We'll answer their questions and then get the hell out of here. I've had enough of this place as it is. And I'm sure Adeline got what she wanted out of this whole debacle."

Olivia and Brock left the body in the house and called the police from the driveway. It took a while for the police to arrive, and then they spent the next few hours of the day answering questions about what had happened. They explained all about the Gamemaster and how they were sure she was the killer, but that she was about as easy to catch as smoke. The police were very interested in their testimony, though Olivia was glad they had credentials on hand to ensure that they were taken seriously. The story was wild and she knew that if they weren't in the FBI, they would never be believed. After everything they'd seen and done, Olivia was starting to feel like she was a little crazy anyway. She hoped that feeling would go away with time, but she knew better than to hope when it came to dealing with the depraved.

By the time the police took over the crime scene, the twenty-four hours were still far from over, but their involvement was done. Olivia and Brock got back in their car and headed off to find somewhere to lay their heads for the night. They still hadn't heard from Adeline, who presumably didn't have a way to spy on them for once, or hadn't bothered to rig the house with cameras for her own viewing pleasure. Olivia and Brock took a nap while they waited for her call, and when it finally came through, it was nighttime. Olivia sat up groggily from her long sleep and picked up the call.

"Sleeping on the job, were you?" Adeline asked Olivia with a sly smile. Olivia scowled at her as Brock woke up beside her.

"Don't act so innocent. We found your Aunt Teresa hours ago. But I'm sure you knew that. And you know that she was long dead before we even arrived."

"Of course she was. I didn't want there to be any chance of her actually surviving this thing. When I want someone dead, they die, Olivia. I'm not the kind of person to wait around and hope that things happen to go my way. So yes, I had her killed a while back. I just wanted to make sure there would be someone there to find the body," Adeline said sweetly.

"The game was rigged. If we never stood a chance, then what was the point in us even being there?" Brock snapped.

"I just told you. You were the cleanup service, essentially. It gave me plenty of time to commit the crime and get out of there before anyone realized what had happened. Not that anyone was looking for that witch. I doubt she has any friends, given the fact that she's mean as hell. Or was, I should say. Plus, it gave you something to do, didn't it? I wanted you to feel useful. I'm sure that's not a feeling you have very often."

"And you don't feel a shred of guilt? For killing a member of your family?" Olivia asked. Adeline rolled her eyes.

"Olivia, did you read that diary? Did you *see* the things she put me through? Of course I don't feel guilty. She made my life hell. Do you have any idea the kind of trauma she put me through as a kid? No, I don't suppose you do. You grew up in a nice house with a nice family and you never had to wonder what it would be like to be beaten up on a daily basis by your parents. Did you?"

"No, but—"

"Then don't try and tell me how to feel about it. I dealt with this the only way I knew how. And if you think I'm crazy, then maybe you should consider the fact that my upbringing wasn't exactly easy. I am what I am. Aunt Teresa made sure that I never stood a chance in this world. So I was just paying back everything that she made me suffer. At least she went with some dignity. I could have tortured her, the way I've been torturing you guys. I'd say that she got the better end of the stick, really. It was quick … not painless, but quick. That's more than she deserved from me."

"Listening to you trying to justify yourself is insane," Brock said, shaking his head in irritation. "You should hear yourself."

"Oh, I do hear myself. Loud and clear. And I believe in everything I'm saying," Adeline said. "Walk a mile in my shoes, Brock. Then maybe you'll get it."

"You know, my life hasn't been so great either. I didn't get much out of my family either. My own grandfather sold me out. So I do know something about the way you're feeling. But I would still never do the things you've done," Brock said. Adeline's lips quirked into a smile.

"Well, I suppose that just makes me the more interesting one out of the two of us," she said. Olivia shook her head.

"I was starting to feel a little bit sorry for you … reading about your childhood, seeing what you had to put up with," Olivia said. "But that was careless of me. I have to remember exactly who you are and what you're capable of."

"Yep. Never forget who I am, Olivia. I certainly won't," Adeline said. "I'll be causing chaos until the end of my days, Olivia."

"What happened to your early retirement plans?" Brock asked with a raised eyebrow. Adeline shrugged.

"I guess I'm too ambitious to give up so easily. But enough about me. I'm going to give you a little time to recuperate. I'm adding some final adjustments to your next task, and you absolutely sped through my murder house! I'll be back in touch in forty-eight hours with your next location. While you're in my hometown, I suggest you head out for dinner at the local Italian. My parents used to take me when I was a child … whenever they actually made time for me. The food is good, and I guess it would add a little romance to your clearly boring lives. Don't say I don't do anything for you. See you soon!"

Adeline hung up the call, and as if on cue, Brock's stomach let out a loud rumble. He sighed.

"I guess we should check it out."

Olivia smiled ever so slightly. "I never thought we would be taking restaurant recommendations from a serial killer."

"There's a first time for everything, right?"

CHAPTER EIGHTEEN

THE ITALIAN RESTAURANT IN TOWN WAS SMALL AND quaint, with fairy lights on the outside. It was practically empty when Olivia and Brock showed up, looking a little worse for wear and not dressed for a date night. Still, Olivia felt grateful to have a little time to recuperate and unwind with Brock. After the things they'd been put through lately, a proper sit-down dinner together was exactly what they needed.

"Table for two, please," Brock said to the waiter as they entered. They were led to a nice table by the window and immediately offered wine, which Olivia accepted. One glass wouldn't hurt, she figured. It might even help to settle her frayed nerves. She still couldn't get the image of Aunt Teresa out of her mind. The day spent at Adeline's old family home had been one of the worst parts of the whole ordeal so far. Not because it was worse than a kidnapped child or a man's corpse being burned in his own store, but because it had almost led Olivia astray. It had almost got her believing that they were dealing with a rational human being, a person who was simply broken by life and had walked off the path. That seemed ridiculous now that she really thought about it. Of course, Adeline was a monster. There was nothing redeemable about her. Had she really become so soft that she believed a child's diary excused the adult she had become? The woman who had killed so many, the woman who had brainwashed Yara and tortured her and Brock for months?

Olivia's thoughts were interrupted by Brock's hand resting on top of hers across the table. She allowed her eyes to drift to meet his.

"Don't think about it," Brock told her softly. "Put it all out of your mind for a while."

Olivia chuckled softly. "I don't think I know how to do that anymore. This is our life, Brock. It's taken over us."

"I know. This last year has been… a lot. But hey… it's also been another whole year of us being together. That's something to celebrate, right?"

"I guess I can raise a glass to that," Olivia said with a smile. She clinked her wine glass against Brock's and took a sip. The red wine was good, and Olivia let out a small sigh. It was a moment of reprieve. It allowed her to relax in her chair and forget her woes for a moment. And when she looked up at Brock, he was smiling at her. She cocked her head to the side.

"What?"

"How do you still manage to be so beautiful after a day like today?" Brock asked her. She felt her cheeks heat up as she blushed.

"You're full of crap."

"That may be true, but I'm serious. You always look perfect."

Olivia chuckled. "Well, it's a good thing you think so. You're kind of stuck with me at this point. But really? Even after all this time?"

"You certainly look perfect to me. But maybe I see you through rose-colored glasses…maybe you're actually a complete slob, a nightmare to look at and even worse to spend time with. Maybe you've put me under some kind of spell. But I don't mind. It's not so bad from my point of view."

Olivia rolled her eyes, which made Brock grin. It was this kind of easy banter that Olivia loved most about their relationship. Sometimes, when their cases were too intense or they let the stress of it all take over, she felt like she missed this. The way they were when there was nothing else standing in their way. But it never took long for them to return to the paradise they always brought to each other's lives. It made all of the rest of it—the stress, the fear, the uncertainty—feel worth it every time.

"Do you think we'll get back to this? When she's gone?" Olivia asked, leaning a little closer to Brock across the table. He ran his thumb over her knuckles, not meeting her eye.

"I hope so. We deserve this. We deserve to be happy. But I don't see her going down easily. After what she said today…"

"That she has more ambition now? That she doesn't want to retire?"

"Yeah, that. That's kind of messed us up, right? Because she said she would stop all this if we played by her rules. But I guess it was naive of us to believe that in the first place."

"Yeah, perhaps a little. But that's the thing with Adeline Clarke. She messes with your mind. She would be so bored if she ever decided to stop. And even if we find her and capture her… who's to say that she won't find some way to escape prison a second time? She's so clever. She always finds a way to worm her way out of any situation."

"Maybe. But we have to try to be positive. We can only focus on doing our end of the job. Our task is to find her and catch her.

We're three tasks down. Only two more and we should be face to face with her. But we have to be ready for anything."

"Agreed. Even if it means that she might wind up dead instead of in prison, we can't risk it a second time, can we? We have to make sure that she never harms anyone again."

They sat there in silence, letting the statement sit, knowing that there was no escaping it. Adeline wasn't likely to walk away from this one alive if she wasn't willing to play by the rules. They both knew that. They couldn't allow other people to die because she'd slipped through their fingers again. Adeline had made too many bad decisions, and now, the world would prefer to see her dead than in prison, especially given all the attention she had brought to herself. She might have some loyal fans left, those who remembered the craziness of the island games with fondness, unscarred by it because they didn't have to live through it.

But Olivia relived those games in her mind every single day. She remembered those who had died, and those who had survived with a new suitcase full of trauma to lug around. Most of all, she remembered how it had destroyed Yara. She had once been a bright spark, a beautiful actress with everything ahead of her. She was just coming back from the shadows of addiction, ready to face the world and start fresh. And now she was a woman on the run, a killer, ruined by Adeline's cruelty.

There was no denying it.

The world would be better off without Adeline Clarke.

"I'm sorry," Brock said. Olivia frowned.

"For what?"

"I'm just sorry. For everything you've had to go through. Everything *we've* been through. And I'm sorry that Adeline isn't a better person. Someone that you can actually see the good in. Because I know you tried today. You wanted to believe that she had redeeming qualities, and that's the goodness in you talking. I'm sorry that she disappointed you."

Olivia sighed. "No, it's okay. It was ridiculous of me to think she could be anything more than a killer. I never should've let my emotions cloud the way. It won't happen again. I promise I know exactly what she is and what she's capable of. I won't let her get in my head and ruin things."

Brock squeezed her hand. "You're too good for this line of work sometimes, Olivia. Adeline never deserved your sympathy."

"I guess I just figured that someone had to see something positive in her... but I've lost sight of that now anyway. The way she so callously played us today... I know better now."

"You were willing to fight in her corner, weren't you? At least a little?"

"Maybe."

"Take that energy and put it where it belongs. With me. You've been fighting in my corner ever since we met, Olivia. Remember that. Remember all that time and care you put into building this thing between us. You don't need to defend a killer. It's just you and I that matter in this world. This is what we can trust. This is what we can protect."

Olivia nodded firmly, squeezing Brock's hand back. "I know. You and me against the world. That's what matters."

Brock raised her hand to his lips and kissed her knuckle.

"I love you more than I ever thought was possible, babe. You've shown me what life is all about. And someday soon, when the storm has passed, I'm going to lock this down for good. I'm going to buy you the ring you deserve, and I'm going to give you forever. And we won't need to steal moments like this in the middle of cases. We won't have to live out of motels and burger joints. We'll have a life together. Just you and me."

Olivia swallowed, feeling a lump in her throat. She'd never heard Brock speak so deeply and honestly. And it felt good to hear it. It was everything she'd been hoping for. The thought of marrying him made her chest warm with love. She smiled at him, holding onto his hand for dear life.

"That sounds absolutely perfect. But just so you know, I'm willing to wait. I know we'll have that life someday. And that makes me happier than I've ever been in my life. But for now, we can carry on kicking ass and saving lives. Because we were born to do this, too. The country needs us. And as long as I'm doing this alongside you, I'm content."

"I know that," Brock murmured. "But the world can wait too. We deserve our moment in the sun. And it's coming soon, I promise you. Just a little longer and we'll have the world in the palm of our hands."

Olivia laid her hand flat on the table, Brock's hand resting on top of her palm. She smiled.

"I already do."

CHAPTER NINETEEN

O LIVIA AND BROCK SLEPT WELL FOR THE FIRST TIME IN A while after their Italian meal and wine. Olivia had to admit Adeline had given them a good recommendation. She felt refreshed even before she had a long shower, but dread returned to her heart as soon as she was dressed. They were about to discover their next challenge, and Olivia was almost sure that the closer they got to the end of the Gamemaster's tasks, the harder they would become. She didn't want to even begin to imagine what might be in store for them for the fourth task. She pictured that it would be grizzly and confusing and that there was a high possibility someone would wind up dead by the end of it.

Brock stepped out of the shower with a yawn, lazily pulling on pants while Olivia sat waiting by her phone.

"You're torturing yourself right now," Brock told her. "The Gamemaster works on her own schedule. I think you should just try and relax until she—"

The phone began to ring, making Olivia jump. Brock let out a sigh.

"She has impeccable timing, doesn't she? You don't think she can see me right now, do you? I'm half naked."

"Good as she is, I don't think she could possibly have found a way to rig our hotel room with cameras… she didn't even know we would be here."

"I still wouldn't put it past her. The devil never rests, after all."

"Get some clothes on. I'll see what she wants."

Olivia picked up the video call, trying not to sigh as Adeline's pretty face came into view. She smiled at Olivia.

"On your own today? Did Brock finally get sick of you and run off with a younger woman?"

Olivia ignored the jibe. The Gamemaster failed to get under her skin in quite the same way that she got under Brock's.

"I'd like to see him try. I'm guessing you've got the next task prepared for us?"

"Oh boy, have I got a treat for you today, Olivia. I think you're really going to enjoy this. I've decided to give you a choice."

Olivia didn't like the sound of that at all. An ultimatum was never good, but when it was playing with people's lives, it was even worse. If she made the wrong decision, would someone end up dead? Was there a moral right or wrong answer? She had no clue what the Gamemaster had come up with this time, but she was certain that she wasn't going to enjoy a second of it.

"What choices do we have?"

"It's very simple. I have two tasks for you to pick from. I won't tell you anything about either task other than its title until you've made a choice. There is a different person held captive for each of the tasks. Whichever task you pick, the other captive will automatically be set free. So no harm done!"

"You say that as if we can trust you to let the person go."

"Scout's honor!"

Olivia narrowed her eyes. "I highly doubt you were a Girl Scout."

"Ugh. Whatever. Consider it my apology for the ways I've messed you around so far. But don't think I'm being over-generous! Whichever task you pick will be very difficult, and I suspect you might face some pretty big obstacles for this one. So yes, one victim will be let go without any consequences... but I bet you won't stand a chance of winning whichever one you pick. These ones are some of my most devious yet."

Olivia chewed the inside of her cheek. How was she supposed to make a decision like this? Even if Adeline was telling the truth about letting one of the victims go, she was also likely condemning one of them to death. That made it an impossible choice. She knew nothing about the victims either, so there was no way of knowing if one of the victims deserved to be set free more than another. But even if she did have that kind of information, would she really feel better? Even if one was a criminal and one was an ordinary person, she still would struggle to make the choice between two human lives.

"What are the choices?" Olivia asked eventually. She hoped that the titles of the tasks might help to sway her decision. Brock arrived at her side just as she asked the question.

"What's going on?"

"You're about to select one of two tasks to complete," Adeline said. "The other will be discarded, which is a shame, but we only have time to play one, I think! There is one person to save in each scenario. Whichever one you don't pick, I'll allow the victim to walk free. So here are your choices. Choice number one... The Heist! Or choice number two... The Maze! Both sound cool, right? Which one are you going to pick? I'll give you a minute to decide between yourselves...but don't keep me waiting for too long or I'll pick for you!"

Olivia turned to Brock, her heart hammering against her chest.

"How the hell are we supposed to pick?"

"I don't know... I'm sure both will be equally awful. But a heist... that sounds like it could involve illegal activity. Like breaking into somewhere and stealing something, maybe. I don't think that's a sensible choice. These games are getting us into enough trouble as it is, and I don't want to have to risk putting ourselves in danger."

"Okay, so...does that mean you want to pick The Maze?"

Brock sighed, throwing his arms up in frustration. "I wouldn't say I want to pick it... but we have to pick one. And at least this will be our choice. What do you think?"

"I guess so... we don't have much of a choice, do we?"

Olivia and Brock turned back to the camera, where Adeline was drumming her fingers impatiently, clearly excited to get on with the task. She raised her eyebrows at them.

"Well? Have you made your final choice? There's no going back once you lock this in, you know. I hope you've picked wisely!"

"Don't try to mind game us now. You've been listening. You know we picked The Maze," Brock said shortly. Olivia hoped that it was the right choice to have made. Who knew? Maybe the titles of the tasks were completely meaningless. Olivia wouldn't put it past the Gamemaster to play them that way.

But they'd made their decision now. They couldn't change it. Adeline tutted.

"Honestly, I hoped you'd pick The Heist... that one was ingenious. But The Maze will be fun, too. Okay, let me put in the word to have the victim set free from the other task... you just saved my math tutor from a world of pain."

Olivia's eyes widened, and Adeline cackled.

"I'm kidding, I'm kidding. It was just some random man I had a bad date with a few years ago. He's safe now, thanks to you! But I guess that means the other unlucky fellow is about to get involved in a game like no other. Are you ready to play?"

"Yes," Olivia said firmly. *Let's get this over with,* she thought.

"Alright then. Step outside of your hotel, if you don't mind. There's a car waiting to take you to the starting location of your task."

"How the hell do you know where we're staying?" Brock snapped. "I told you she was spying on us..."

Adeline rolled her eyes. "Of course, I'm spying on you, Brock. I've been planning this for months. But this is the only hotel in town. *That's* how I know where to find you. I'm not that much of a genius. Now hurry up. My driver doesn't like to be kept waiting."

The call ended, and Olivia sighed, grabbing her bag and pulling Brock out of the hotel and downstairs. Sure enough, a sleek black car was parked in front of the hotel; the windows blacked out so they couldn't see inside. Olivia cautiously opened the door to the back of the vehicle, and Brock climbed in after her. There was a partition, so they couldn't see who their driver was, but whoever it was began to drive the moment the doors were closed.

They waited in tense silence as they weaved through the town. But when minutes of driving turned to an hour, Olivia began to wonder where on earth they were going. She wanted to ask the driver, but she was sure that secrecy was a part of the task. She couldn't even see out of the window to guess at where they were going to end up. Brock held her hand, but he too, seemed to be pondering where they were going and what was about to happen to them. Who knew what they would be about to face?

Only the Gamemaster.

The car eventually came to a complete stop. The driver said nothing, but with the engine killed, Olivia assumed it was time for them to exit the car. As they stepped out, a manila folder was tossed out of the passenger side window, and then the car drove off before Olivia could protest. She scrambled to the ground to pick up the folder before anything blew away. As her fingers closed around it, she realized she was standing on a pretty busy road. A car honked at her, and she scrambled back to the sidewalk, her heart thrumming in her ears.

"I guess this is the task," she said, sliding a single piece of paper out of the folder. On it was a diagram.

The image showed a maze, drawn by hand in black ink. Each corridor was made to look like a hedge.

But it was more complicated than any maze Olivia had ever seen before. It didn't help that each of the corridors was tiny and intricate. It didn't even have an obvious place to enter the maze or a central point that made much sense. She stared at it, wondering what the hell the image meant and what they were supposed to do with it. But there was nothing else in the folder or on the back of the piece of paper. They had nothing else to work with.

"Did the Gamemaster say how long we have to complete this task?" Olivia asked. Brock shook his head.

"No... but let's assume we're racing against the clock. We usually are."

Olivia looked up to the sky. They'd been in the car a long while, and the sun was beginning to dip. It was late afternoon. Her stomach was rumbling—they hadn't had a chance to eat before they left the hotel.

She handed the sheet of paper over to Brock.

"Can you make any sense of this at all?

He stared at it for a minute or two. Then he shook his head.

"I have no idea. I mean, obviously this is the maze. It has to be important. But we don't even know where we are. Any clues?"

"Well, we were in the car for a few hours at least... I lost track of the time a little. We went through New York, I think, but we don't even know which direction we drove in. We could be anywhere by now. It looks like we're pretty far from the city, though... check on your phone maps."

Olivia looked around, hoping to find some sort of familiar landmark, but even the tall skyscrapers of Manhattan were simply too far away from where they stood.

"Know of any mazes in Upstate New York?" she asked hopefully, knowing the question was ridiculous even as she said it. "Not my area of expertise, unfortunately. But let's be honest, it's not going to be as simple as finding a maze. No, this picture *means* something. We just have to figure out what." Brock paused and smiled. "You know what helps me think?"

Olivia sighed. "Alright. Let's go and grab a burger and figure this out."

CHAPTER TWENTY

O LIVIA AND BROCK SAT SIDE BY SIDE IN THE DINER, waiting for their orders to arrive as they examined the drawn-out picture of the maze. Olivia really had never seen anything like it. There were so many twists and turns in the maze's layout and the angles of the avenues made the whole thing even more difficult to navigate. She couldn't imagine it being real in any practical way, and she was certain that whatever they were looking at wasn't a literal maze. There had to be something more to what they were seeing in front of them.

Olivia placed her finger on the outer edge and tried to make her way to the center of the maze, but even once she'd managed it, she didn't really understand what the point of it was. The avenues themselves actually made an easy enough path to the slightly off-center middle of the maze, a blank space that connected to about five or six of the pathways. There were plenty of ways to get to the blank space in the middle, so Olivia was sure that they would be able to use the image easily to navigate their way to *somewhere*. The trouble was figuring out what it meant. Where was the maze and what was its actual purpose?

"Any ideas?" Olivia asked. Brock sipped on his soda thoughtfully, in the zone now that he was about to be fed and happy. Olivia supposed she should always have Brock working from a diner if she wanted him to be functioning at maximum brainpower. But she didn't have time to make a comment on it, so she moved on.

"I wondered if maybe it's meant to be a blueprint of some kind? A layout for something in this town, possibly. Do you see this lattice-like section in the corner? Where the avenues just cross over one another, almost in a hashtag shape? I thought maybe it might be, like, pipes or something in a building. That was the first thing that popped into my mind when I saw that part. But it just seems too complicated to be a floor plan in a building. And far too big as well. I know it's only a piece of paper, but the intricacy of all of this, all these tiny walkways… it looks like we're dealing with something huge here. Something on a bigger scale than something that can be contained."

"Hmm. Interesting idea, though. Because I'm pretty sure that if we're using this for something, then it's not a literal maze. It feels like this must be a puzzle. Like it's not designed to be used in a totally literal way.."

"That makes sense when we're dealing with the Gamemaster. Logic puzzles are kind of her thing. So what makes this maze special? I mean other than the fact that she clearly drew this by hand. God, she's like a child."

"She practically is a child, Brock. But she thinks like an adult. So this has meaning to it, definitely. Do you think there's any chance we're supposed to rearrange it? There are no dead ends, so that would be difficult to imagine, but maybe we're supposed to find one true path to the middle. There's six ways to reach the center at least, judging by how many walkways come out of it."

"Maybe… but maybe we're overcomplicating it. If we look at it simply as it is… is there a way to give it meaning?"

"I mean, if we simplify it, then the basic idea is to get to somewhere, presumably where we will find the victim. And if we follow these avenues somewhere in a literal manner… maybe these are actual directions. Maybe we have to find a starting point and try to move through the city as if we were following a…"

Olivia had a thought that rushed over her so fast that her heart skipped a beat. She stood up and edged out of the booth.

"Where are you going?" Brock called after her.

"I'll be back!"

It only took ten minutes for Olivia to find what she was looking for and come back with the item she needed. She laid it out on the table proudly, showing Brock. His forehead creased.

"You want to go sightseeing?"

"The maze is a *map*, Brock. I had to buy a paper one so we can figure out where the maze corresponds to. But look, here's Hudson Springs, which is apparently where we are. And if we put the piece of paper over the top of the city map…"

Olivia had to turn the sheet of paper several times to get the desired effect she wanted, but it worked. It wasn't quite to scale— the maze had been amplified more than on the map to make the avenues clearer—but when Olivia arranged it on top of the map, it became obvious that the roads matched to the avenues on the maze drawing. And if Olivia adjusted the maze a little more, she could see exactly where the center of the maze was meant to be.

"That's… that's the football stadium," Brock said. "This can't be right… surely the Gamemaster hasn't somehow broken into a huge public stadium to hide a person there? I mean, how do you even hide someone in a stadium other than in complete plain sight? And how long can she possibly keep the victim there for? We still don't even know how much time we have to figure this out!"

"We know the Gamemaster loves the grand scale of things," Olivia said. "I think she's using this as a chance to show off. She might have found a way to get inside at night once everyone has left... I'm sure it would have been easy to bribe the groundskeeper somehow. And if the victim is going to be at the stadium in the middle of the night, then we'll have to go there after it closes."

Brock groaned. "So we're going to have to break in to a place anyway."

"It's definitely not ideal. But I get the impression that calling the cops is another big no-no for this task. We know how the Gamemaster felt about us getting other people involved... it takes this whole thing national and we can't afford to make her angry ahead of the last task. It'll only make things worse if we don't keep this on the down low."

"Is it possible that we're wrong about this? The map isn't to scale, we might have got the proportions wrong..."

"No, I don't think so. This drawing is pretty accurate when you line it up. And look... if we pinpoint the place where we were dropped off, it's at the start of one of the avenues that lead to the center. I'm certain of this one. The Gamemaster wants to draw us there. It almost feels like the maze isn't the big surprise. I think there's going to be something there to make this more of a challenge. Maybe the stadium itself is a metaphorical maze... I mean, it's a lot of ground to cover. And if we don't have long to find the victim, then I suppose that ups the ante, doesn't it?"

"It does. If I could venture a guess, I would think that the Gamemaster knows that we have to do this before the staff show up again tomorrow. Which means that tonight is the night, or we'll fail. And I think she didn't tell us a time limit so we'd have to work it out for ourselves. Which makes the entire thing more stressful again. That seems like the kind of thing that she would try to put us through, doesn't it?"

147

"Well, I definitely feel a lot less positive about this task now that you've put it that way," Olivia said. "But if she's speeding up the timeline for us once again then I'm not complaining... this whole thing could be over by tomorrow at this rate. That can only be a good thing, right?"

Brock took a steadying breath. "Wouldn't that be sweet? I'm still waiting for some kind of bigger twist, though. None of this has been simple, and I doubt it's about to start now."

"Then enjoy this meal while we can," Olivia said as she saw the waitress arriving with their burgers. "I think we've got a long night ahead of us."

CHAPTER
TWENTY-ONE

O LIVIA AND BROCK DISCOVERED THAT THE STADIUM was closed from ten pm onward on the day of their break-in plans. Starting at the point where they had been dropped off, they spent an hour walking to the stadium, just in case the Gamemaster was finicky about them actually following the layout of the maze she'd drawn out. By the time they arrived there, night was falling, and all they had to do was find an opening to get inside.

They waited outside the stadium, watching as all the workers trickled out until no one appeared to be left. Then, silently, they got closer to see what they were dealing with.

There was no simple way to get inside. There were automatic doors at the entrance that had been locked, and then any other entrances were for workers only, needing a special access card to enter. But they took an opportunity when they saw a lone janitor heading out for a smoke break, stealing in through the propped-open employee entrance.

"There's still people around," Brock hissed to Olivia as soon as they were inside and out of earshot. "What if someone sees us?"

"I think we've got bigger things to worry about than being spotted by a janitor," Olivia said, her shoes squeaking on the polished floors of the corridors. "We can play that off if we need to. Besides, they'll be glad we're here if things start to go downhill. We're the only ones around to protect any civilians from whatever the Gamemaster has planned. What we need to know is where the hell the Gamemaster has hidden the victim. Because if we don't find them soon, it's possible they'll wind up dead."

"It's nearly eleven," Brock said, checking his watch. "Nothing seems off right now, but maybe she's waiting for something in particular. Do you think something will happen at midnight?"

"I certainly wouldn't put it past the Gamemaster to put on a show. She does love her theatrics, so midnight would certainly be poetic. And to make it happen here, in a huge stadium... she's really been planning ahead."

"I still don't know what she could possibly pull off in such a small amount of time."

"Don't underestimate her. We both know what she's capable of. And if we take our eye off the ball, that's when she'll find a way to take us down when we least expect it. Keep your eyes peeled."

Olivia checked the gun on her belt. The Gamemaster hadn't said anything about them being unarmed, so she assumed it wasn't against the rules. If it was, she guessed she would deal with the consequences later, but any victim who was waiting to be saved would be much safer if she was armed. That logic alone was enough to make her feel comfortable with her decision.

They didn't see anyone else as they scoured the perimeter of the place. If the Gamemaster had any other lackeys working in the stadium, they didn't stumble across them. They also didn't see any other janitors or onsite workers, which Olivia took as a sign that Adeline had managed to bribe them all for the night. Now, anything felt as though it was possible.

The place was completely silent, devoid of the usual hustle and bustle of stadium life. They searched as thoroughly as they could, checking in kiosks for signs of anything suspicious, but there wasn't anything amiss. They checked every bathroom and Olivia had horrible deja vu from searching the FBI headquarters for the bomb the Gamemaster had planted and eventually finding the victim in the toilets. But there was nothing in any of the bathrooms except one abandoned janitor cart.

"I'll bet the Gamemaster has paid the janitors off. Made them leave early so that she can set up whatever she has planned," Olivia mused. "And it looks like nothing is happening indoors…"

"We could check the VIP boxes," Brock pointed out. "But I think we both know where something is most likely to happen."

Olivia nodded. "Out on the field."

She had no doubt about that. The Gamemaster lived for drama. If something was going to happen, it would likely be at midnight, right on the fifty-yard line. The rest just felt like killing time. She sighed, shaking her head to herself. They'd nearly wasted an entire hour checking out the perimeter. It was time to face up to what they needed to do.

"We should head out there."

Brock nodded. They headed for the locker rooms, finding them unlocked. Then, just before midnight, they headed through the tunnel and out onto the field.

It was completely dark at first as they walked out. Olivia couldn't see a thing, no matter how hard she squinted her eyes.

And then it began.

The floodlights came on a few at a time, metallically thrumming as they came alive. Olivia shielded her eyes, suddenly blinded. They were so bright that everything felt a little surreal. But Olivia could still see something coming into view.

In the center of the field, someone was tied to a chair, bound so tightly that they couldn't move. Olivia knew this had to be the Gamemaster's unfortunate victim.

They had to get to the person fast.

And then the fireworks started. Someone had lit them close to the victim, so close that they could easily have exploded and hurt the victim. They shot into the sky with loud bangs, color splattering against a sky painted white by the stadium lights.

Olivia's head whipped around as music began to blare through speakers. They'd gone from complete sensory deprivation to an overload like no other. It was so loud that it felt as though it was thrumming inside Olivia's eardrums. But Olivia was sure it was all smoke and mirrors. A distraction from what was truly happening around them. They couldn't afford to let it turn their focus.

"We need to help them," Olivia cried out, her voice lost in the music as she set off at a run toward the victim. She could see now, as she got closer, that it was a terrified young man dressed in a janitorial uniform. *So much for paying the janitors off,* Olivia thought. And the next set of fireworks was a little too close for comfort, sitting very close to the chair. There was no one to light them, but Olivia suspected they might be remotely controlled. If they exploded, it might not kill the man, but it would certainly injure him very badly. There was no telling when they would be set off. Without thinking what she was risking, Olivia launched herself toward the chair, toppling it out of the way just as the fireworks exploded around her ears.

There was a blast of heat close to her as the fireworks shot up, but she was just out of range. She heard the muffled cry of the janitor, Olivia's weight pressing the chair on top of him, but she knew his fate could've been much worse. Feeling a little dizzy from the proximity of the explosion, she stumbled to her feet, trying to get the chair back upright so she could untie the janitor.

She had no idea what else the Gamemaster might've set up for them there, but she didn't want to stick around to find out. She planned to untie the man and then just get out.

But as she was untying the complex knots holding the janitor, she saw movement in the stands. At first, she thought it was the blinding lights making her see shadows, but then she saw a figure running down past the seats, barreling toward the field. Brock hadn't clocked whoever it was, still looking blindly for trouble elsewhere.

"Brock!" Olivia cried hoarsely, but her voice was lost in the blaring music and the concussions of the fireworks. She could do nothing as she watched the figure vault the barrier, slamming straight into Brock and taking him down.

"I'll be back!" Olivia cried to the terrified janitor, setting off on a run. She could see Brock wrestling the man on the ground. The glint of a knife shone in the darkness, and Olivia suddenly realized who the person was.

The assassin.

They'd been warned that someone would hunt them down, but as she watched Brock fight back, pushing the man off of him, she wondered what kind of assassin was only armed with a knife. He fought skillfully, his knife whipping back and forth in moves that would kill anyone ordinary in an instant. But Brock was equipped for the fight, taking only a few nicks on his arms as he fended off the attack with quick, calculated steps. He'd done this dance before, and he wasn't about to let this man take him down. He was also buying Olivia enough time to get there and disarm the assassin.

Olivia managed to grab her gun from her belt, but she wasn't going to shoot the assassin. Not before they got information out of him.

She approached rapidly from behind the assassin as he wrestled with Brock. He darted a quick look toward her, but that was the distraction Brock needed. He lunged forward with a quick punch to the gut, while Olivia bore down even faster. Raising her arm, she smacked the gun against the side of the assassin's face, making him stumble. Then, she swept her foot against his ankle, knocking him to the ground.

But while anyone else would be completely floored, the assassin clearly knew how to counter such an attack. He rolled as he fell down and launched himself back to his feet in an instant, knife back at the ready. He was only momentarily shaken and ready for action once again. Olivia raised her gun level with his forehead as a warning.

"Don't make me shoot."

"You may as well," the man growled, launching another attack on her, though she stepped back just in time. "Someone isn't getting out of here alive. If I don't kill you, the Gamemaster will kill me."

He feinted left, but Olivia was ready when he moved on her again, used to these kinds of tricks. She kept her gun steady, and her eyes trained on him, but she didn't shoot. She wanted it to be a last resort.

"The Gamemaster has spilled enough blood. Let's talk about this."

"I'm not much of a talker," the assassin quipped. He moved to slice her throat, but she batted his hand away and twisted his arm hard around his back. He yelped and lost the knife as it clattered to the ground.

"What does she have on you? Why is she making you do this?" Olivia shouted in his ear, still deafened by the music. Almost too late, she realized the was drawing another knife. He whirled around to try and slice her but she jumped aside, letting go of his arm. She really didn't want to hurt him, but the man was relentless. Whatever was going on, he clearly didn't want to back down.

"She's paying off a bounty on my head," the man said, barely breathless as he twirled the new knife between his fingers. "I'm an assassin by trade, and I've got bad people after me. But there's a device strapped to my back. If you walk out of here alive, she'll fry me with an electric shock. This isn't personal. It's just another job. I don't know who you are, and I don't care. But I have to do this if I want to live."

"If she wanted you to kill us, why did she only arm you with a knife?" Olivia asked as the assassin slowed his pace, making a slow arc with his knife to keep Brock and Olivia away from him. The assassin laughed bitterly.

"I guess she doesn't really want me to do it. I knew she wouldn't want to. The bounty on my head is significant, and she's not going to want to fork out for it. Plus, given what she's been putting you through, I figure she's got something worse planned for you than a quick death at my hand. Tonight was my last chance to get this done, but I've been set up to lose this entire time. It's two against one, and you both have guns." He stopped pacing and shook his head to himself. "You know what? It just isn't worth it. You may as well shoot me now. I'm tired of the games."

Brock now had his gun trained on the assassin, too, and they circled him like predators, keeping the assassin on his toes. There was no fear in his eyes, but beads of sweat trickled down his forehead. He was still now, his head hung low.

"You don't have to feel sorry for me. I always knew this ride would end badly," the assassin said, shaking his head. "You don't get into this trade if your life is going well. I don't have anyone to leave behind… no wife, no kids. I live for money, and I'll die for it now, I guess. Just get it over with."

"We don't want to shoot you. Maybe we can help," Brock said, still circling the man. "Can we take a look at the device?"

"No. You can't help me. She'll know," the assassin said through gritted teeth. "Just do me a favor and end it yourself. You'll save me a world of pain. Look, I'll drop the knife. I'm done. I don't have a way out anymore. I don't think I ever did."

"We're not killing an unarmed man," Olivia said firmly. "We'll call the police in. They can deal with you themselves."

"Then you're condemning me anyway," the assassin growled. "Just do it yourself."

"No," Brock said firmly. "You chose this, but you can't force our hand too. The Gamemaster has done that to us enough times. We're in control this time. Put your hands in the air. Olivia, you can go and help the victim."

She nodded, trusting Brock to handle the assassin. He had all but given up anyway. She could understand that. The Gamemaster had that effect on people. Hell, she had been pushed to that point a few times in the last year. But she would never truly give up. Not while there was still breath in her body.

And that was the only reason she had survived the Gamemaster for so long. Her resilience was something Adeline hadn't counted on. Maybe that was why she was so obsessed with her and Brock. She wanted them to break, but no matter what she threw at them, they just kept getting back up.

She found the victim sobbing, still tied up on the chair. The fireworks were over now, and the music had stopped. Wherever the Gamemaster was, she surely knew that they'd won another task. Olivia hushed the young janitor as she worked to untie him.

"It's going to be okay. You're safe now," she promised. But she couldn't help feeling that the end of the fourth task meant something more ominous for her and Brock. A final task that was worthy to compete with everything they had faced so far.

A task that would finish them off.

CHAPTER TWENTY-TWO

THE ASSASSIN DIDN'T STRUGGLE AS THE POLICE TOOK HIM away. Olivia and Brock were as patient as they could manage as they explained that while they had broken into stadium unlawfully, they did it to save the young janitor's life. It turned out that the janitor had indeed received a healthy bribe from the Gamemaster, but when he refused to go through with the bargain, he became a victim of Adeline's games. The other four janitors who had been on shift that night had now disappeared, presumably with a lot of money in their pockets.

The janitor had been nothing but thankful to Olivia and Brock for what they had done, but Olivia had bigger things on her mind by the time the police finally allowed them to leave. The sunrise was arriving, and Olivia felt exhausted, but she knew that it was only a matter of time before the final task was underway. Now that the fourth task was out of the way, the Gamemaster would be ramping up to whatever horrors she had in store for Olivia and Brock at the end of her games. It was the beginning of the end, which kept her going more than anything else. There was a nervous energy thrumming in her veins as the promise of freedom from the Gamemaster loomed a little closer.

"Well, that was an experience at least," Brock said, suppressing a yawn as they headed back through the city to find somewhere to hire a car. "And another victim saved from the Gamemaster and her tasks."

"Yeah," Olivia said with a sigh. "But yet another life ruined by her too."

"If you mean the assassin, then you shouldn't feel sorry for him. He didn't have to come after us, he did it to save his own skin. He knew he wasn't a good person, but, he kept choosing the wrong path anyway. He made his choice," Brock said, folding his arms defensively. Olivia raised an eyebrow.

"We're doing pretty much the same thing that he is. Doing what she tells us so that we can stop something awful happening to us."

"Except the difference is that we're trying to save people, not kill them. We have been going out of our way to search for and save people we know nothing about. Even when we tried to save Aunt Teresa, knowing that she had done awful things in her life. And then we let the assassin live. We could've killed him on the spot for what he was trying to do. It would have counted as self-defense."

"And it sounded like that's what he wanted us to do. Kill him, I mean. It was preferable to what the Gamemaster would do to him now. He said something about a device on his back … what if she's already set off some kind of kill switch? What if he's dead before he even makes it to prison?"

Brock wavered, looking uncomfortable. "He tried to force us to shoot him, Olivia. If you were willing to do that, then fair enough, but I certainly wasn't. I've seen enough death caused by the Gamemaster's antics. I wasn't going to end his life just because he wanted to escape the deal he made with her. That's not on us."

Olivia didn't try to argue further. She knew that neither of them was about to kill that man, no matter what he was willing to do to them. It went against everything they stood for, and even if he had gotten on his knees and begged, Olivia would never have been able to go through it. But Brock seemed determined to hate the guy when it was clear he'd just taken a few wrong turns in his lifetime. He had become a killer because he had nothing else to do with himself, but maybe in another life, he might have been okay. Olivia thought that anyone could've ended up in his shoes if their life went wrong somewhere down the line. She thought about all the things she'd been through in the past few years—losing her sister, her mother's disappearance, more near-death experiences than she cared to count. If she had let those things ruin her the way she thought they would, then she could've ended up doing something bad. With her experience in the FBI, she could easily have walked into the same line of work as the assassin clearly had. Only her perseverance stood between her and a miserable alternate timeline. That's how simple she thought it was—the balance between good and evil choices wasn't as weighted as many liked to believe.

And the more Olivia thought about it, the more the assassin reminded her of someone. Yara. She had made a wrong turn, too. When her alcoholism had made her lose all of her senses, she had fallen straight into Adeline Clarke's open arms, willing to do anything to survive. That single choice that she had made meant that she tumbled down and down into a pit of bad decisions. Since then, she had killed, tortured, lied, and broken promises. She had made every poor choice in the book. All because she had a moment of weakness.

Now, she was stuck beside Adeline while she tortured them. Maybe that's why Brock was so angry about the whole thing. Maybe the assassin reminded him of Yara and everything she had done to him. In his eyes, there was no good where evil lay too. There was no chance of redemption when there were so many other paths that could be taken before throwing a life away.

That's how he'd felt about Yara ever since the island. He'd barely mentioned her name in weeks, even while they were facing the Gamemaster face on, but Olivia knew that his old friend had to be on his mind more than ever. Would they see her again in the final task? Would he ever be able to tell her just how much she had hurt them?

Olivia had no idea what would happen next, but she hoped it would be over with fast. She was growing weary of all the running around, never knowing if they would survive the next task. But Olivia had a feeling that the Gamemaster had been going somewhat easy on them. The first task had been bad, but the second? Adeline had allowed them to save a young child. Then for the third task, she had simply played with them a little—the guilt wasn't on them for what had happened to Aunt Teresa, even if they still felt bad about what had happened. Even their most recent task hadn't seemed as threatening as Olivia had expected—their assassin never really stood a chance when he was armed only with a knife. He had never really wanted to kill them in the first place. He was only doing what he needed to survive. And wasn't that a familiar story, given that they were doing the same thing?

But it occurred to Olivia that there was a good reason that the Gamemaster hadn't upped the ante yet. Adeline was preparing to see them again one final time in the grand finale. She'd never get that chance if they hadn't survived the rest of the tasks. Whatever she had in mind for them, Olivia was sure that it would be an absolute nightmare. And there was no chance she was going to risk them not being there to experience it.

Olivia and Brock headed to a small diner to grab coffee and breakfast while they waited for the call from the Gamemaster.

Neither of them spoke much, and even Brock didn't feel like eating. There was an ominous cloud above their heads, warning them of what was about to come their way. The final task would be their chance to finally capture their most elusive and troublesome villain yet. Only when she was caught would they be able to get their lives back in full.

"Whatever happens ... we can't lose our heads," Olivia said to Brock pointedly. He nodded solemnly.

"I know. Whatever she has planned will be designed to drive us crazy. She may even try to turn us on each other. I have no doubt Yara will be there too, as a way to bait me. But I know what we're in for."

"You do have a tendency to lose your cool with the Gamemaster..."

"I don't know how you don't. She has destroyed our lives for so long now that I can barely even remember what life was like before she showed up. She drives me insane."

"She bothers me too. But I know it's different for you. She's made it more personal with you. But she does it because she sees that it bothers you. You can't let her win this time. This is the last time we'll have to face her. At least, in theory. Don't let her get under your skin."

"I won't," Brock said gruffly. "Not this time. Though, it's going to be hard. Especially... especially with Yara involved."

Olivia nodded. "Are you feeling okay? About probably seeing her?"

Brock ran a hand through his hair, looking troubled. "Not really. It's the last thing I need right now. On top of the rest of this pressure ... knowing that she's beyond saving—and has been for a long time—is a lot to cope with. And who knows what the Gamemaster will make her do this time. I don't want anyone else to die at her hand. Even though I'm done with her... even though I can never forgive what she's done to us and to herself... I don't want to see her suffer any further. I don't want to watch her crawl deeper into the hole that the Gamemaster has dug for her."

Olivia nodded. Yara's downfall was truly a tragedy. She'd had it all once. A beautiful home, a fun, exciting career that was only just starting to blossom, and all the privileges she could ever want. But her addiction to alcohol had sent her on a downward spiral. It was hard to remember that when the plane went down on the island where they first encountered the Gamemaster, she had been trying to get away to a spa retreat, to get better.

But she never got the chance. And now she was just another puppet on the Gamemaster's strings. She'd lost her former self almost entirely. She'd killed people. She'd sacrificed her own sanity to stay alive.

She'd ruined every chance she ever had.

Olivia put her hand over Brock's.

"We can't change the past. We can't save her now. I think we have to make a decision now... if it comes down to saving Yara or a civilian... you know what we have to do, don't you?"

Brock nodded curtly, not hesitating for a moment. "Of course. She's in too deep now. It won't be easy to make that choice... but we have to make sure that we protect the innocent. And Yara is far from innocent these days." Brock paused, looking at Olivia with pain in his eyes. "But should it come to that... I might need you to lead the way. I'll need help."

Olivia squeezed his hand. "That's okay."

"Really?"

"Yes, Brock. I cared for Yara, but you knew her for a long time. And I don't want you to have to hurt her if it comes to that."

"I can't... I can't believe you're willing to do that for me," Brock said quietly. Olivia frowned.

"I'd do pretty much anything for you, Brock. You should know that by now."

Brock lowered his eyes, breathing out a heavy sigh. Olivia took the opportunity to lean in and kiss his cheek gently. Her heart felt heavy, knowing that the Gamemaster would be more than willing to throw Yara into the firing line to protect herself. And when that inevitably happened, Yara was going to end up hurt.

At Olivia's hand.

But it was necessary, and if it was a choice between protecting Brock, the man she loved, or Yara, the person who had betrayed them time and time again, she knew who she would choose without a doubt.

They sat in silence for a while until the Gamemaster's call came through. Olivia squeezed Brock's hand one final time and, together, they answered Adeline's call.

"You guys have really knocked it out of the park. I'm impressed," she said as her face showed up on the screen, grinning with pride. "I'm glad you enjoyed my little task. I thought it would be a fun one before the big finale. But what *is* the big finale, you ask?"

"Can't we just get this over with?" Brock asked. Olivia nudged him gently, reminding him to keep his cool. Adeline sighed.

"Alright, alright. Here it is. I'm about to give you a choice. I've given you choices in the past … but make the wrong decision this time, and the victims will die before you even get to try and save them. I'll blow them all sky high. Make the wrong decision, and I'll slip through your fingers once again, never to be seen again. But if you choose correctly… you'll be invited to join me for the final task. You'll have a chance to save multiple lives. And you'll get to be a part of the showdown of the century."

It was all a little too theatrical for Olivia's taste. She felt like she was on a corny game show. Except that there was no grand prize. If they were lucky, they'd get out of there alive. That was the best that they could hope for.

"Here's the choice," the Gamemaster said with a sly smile. "My victims and I are holing up in one of two locations. You must guess where we are and find your way to us. You will be given forty-eight hours to get to the correct location. If you're wrong, then everyone dies. Maybe even me. I haven't decided how seriously to take my suicide pact yet. I mean, if that happens, at least you don't need to do a final task, right? But if you pick the correct location, then everything will go ahead as planned. We will have the big finish that I've been dreaming of for so long…"

Olivia stared at Adeline on the screen in horror. The fact that she was even willing to kill herself terrified Olivia. That meant they were dealing with a woman who had nothing to fear. She shouldn't have been surprised after everything they'd seen her do, but she was.

They had a fifty-fifty chance of getting it right. But that also meant an equal possibility of being completely wrong. Olivia took a deep breath, her lungs feeling constricted. She hoped there might be some logic to the right choice. At least then they stood a chance of making the right decision.

"Are you ready to hear the locations?" Adeline asked with a grin. "Let's not keep the suspense up for any longer. Where will I hold the grand finale? Will it be at my home? Or will it be… on the island?"

Olivia's heart dropped to her stomach. *The island.* The place where it had all began. The place that haunted her dreams. She couldn't bear the thought of having to go back there, of having to relive everything that happened to them while they were there. Not to mention that the entire thing was streamed online, so people could obsess over their survival. Surely Adeline couldn't be serious about that choice?

But of course, she could. This was by far one of her cruelest tricks yet, but it shouldn't be unexpected.

"That's all you're going to tell us?" Brock asked, sounding winded. Adeline cackled madly.

"That's all you get! You must make your way to one or the other within forty-eight hours. I'll be waiting at the correct location. And if you're not there when the time is up… I'll know you've made the wrong decision. I've rigged my current location with bombs. If you don't come, I'll set them off. And all of the victims I have with me will die."

Olivia felt sick to her stomach. She had no idea where they were supposed to go. But Adeline was clearly done with walking them through the whole thing. She waggled her fingers at them on the other side of the camera.

"See you soon…or not."

The video call cut off before they could say anything else. Brock let out a deep sigh, sinking his head into his hands.

"Man, how the hell are we supposed to navigate this one? She's given us a near-impossible choice. One wrong decision… it'll change everything."

Olivia took a deep breath, trying to calm herself.

"We can do this," she said firmly. "We just need to think about this logically. We already have a fifty percent chance of being right. If we apply our minds, we can improve our chances."

"You think she chose how to do this *logically?*"

"Yes. Because it's like I've said this entire time, we've been learning more about her, figuring out how she works. And she does everything for a reason, just like anyone else." Olivia exhaled slowly. "We just have to figure out what that reason is."

CHAPTER
TWENTY-THREE

O LIVIA KNEW THAT THEY DIDN'T HAVE VERY LONG TO
make the decision of where to go. If they were going
to get to the island in time, then they needed to make
travel arrangements to get there, and that wasn't going to be a
quick process. Plus, this wasn't a decision to be made lightly.
Whatever path they chose would have serious consequences
either way and though Olivia hoped that they would know
which option to pick, right at that moment, she felt unsure. As
they got in the car to discuss their options, Olivia took a deep
breath, feeling the weight of the world weighing down on her
shoulders.

This really was a life-or-death situation for someone. Maybe even multiple people.

They had to get it right.

"Okay. Let's give ourselves one hour to make this decision before we make a move. Or else it's going to drive us crazy for two days. That's probably what the Gamemaster is counting on anyway. That the not knowing will be too much for us to handle." She paused and breathed deeply again. These days, she felt she had to concentrate or she might not breathe at all. She rubbed at the tight spot in her chest where tension was never quite released. It hurt, and she hoped that once the games were over, it might dissipate for good.

"So we have two choices... the island or the house. The place where we first met or the place she sent us to last."

"An impossible choice," Brock murmured. "Two places that mean something to her, and one place that truly means something to us. Which is more important to her—taking us somewhere stressful or somewhere that she deems to be meaningful? I can think of reasons why she would host the final task in either of these locations, but I can't for the life of me decide which place outweighs the other. But I'm sure that whichever place she wants us to go to is important to her in some way."

"Is there any way that we can actually work this out, do you think?" Olivia asked Brock. "Do you think maybe she's made a puzzle for us to follow this whole time? Like maybe there's hidden clues in things she's said to us... if we can remember the exact wording of everything she's told us up until now, maybe there are hidden meanings in there. Or is that too much?"

"I don't know," Brock said. "I mean, she does like to mess with us, and creating puzzles for us to solve sounds like something she would do. But I can't think of anything that might be a clue, can you? I also think that the stakes are so high here that she wouldn't be obvious about any clues she did leave. If we read into every single thing she says we'll go crazy, and even then, it's still pretty much fifty-fifty odds of getting it right. I get the feeling that she wants us to scramble around for answers. She wants us to really work for this, and maybe even fail. It's an all or nothing play for her finale, I think. By the way she spoke about it, she plans to kill herself if we don't make it to her location."

"We can't be sure she meant that. She says plenty of things just for the flair of it all. She probably wants us to believe that the stakes are higher than they are. And it's not something we can possibly risk her doing, even if it means being rid of her for good. She said she'd blow up the location, which would kill whoever else is with her right now, including Yara. We don't know how many people's lives are at risk here. She said *victims,* plural. I'll bet that this grand finale has a lot more people at risk than any of the other tasks. The victims have to be our priority, over catching her, even. She might even try to make this personal again… like last time."

Olivia shuddered at the thought, remembering how their friends had been enlisted into the island challenges at the last minute as a way to get at Brock and Olivia. And Jonathan had ended up dead in the end, even if he had made it through the fight on the boat. Yara and the Gamemaster had seen to that. Olivia dreaded to think who else the Gamemaster would drag into this entire mess. The first face that came to her mind was her mother, and it made her wince. She'd almost lost her so many times before. She would be the perfect emotional blackmail target for the Gamemaster to go for, and Olivia wouldn't put it past her to stoop that low. She'd done worse in the past.

"We can't know any of the real details until we actually get there, unfortunately. We're just going to have to work with the facts and leave the speculation off the table. So let's focus on what we can figure out," Brock said. "I think there's two possibilities here. The first is that she wants to take us back to the island to make us relive all of the awful things she did to us there. It's a big, theatrical gesture, which is exactly like something she would do. It would also bring her the kind of attention that she has likely craved ever since the last time she did it. She might've found ways to get the old contestants back there, even, with new games to make it even more awful. It would be insane if she pulled it off, but we know what she is capable of.."

"God, I hope the second option is better than this sounds..."

"The second option is that she will think we'll be drawn to the island more because it means something to us. I know she's smart, but I don't see how she can get away with pulling off the island trick a second time. She probably thinks we'll assume that her main focus is to torture us, and that's why she would make us go back and relive our worst nightmares. But I think you've been right all along, Olivia. You've been taking a closer look at who she is and seeing things that perhaps she *wanted* us to see. This was never about us—it was about her. That's the thing with a woman like Adeline... there's nothing more precious to her than the spotlight."

"How do you mean?"

"The island was the first time she truly revealed herself to the world. Everyone knew who she was when it was happening. But now she's one of the world's most wanted. If she wants to up the ante, she needs to make this more personal. And what's more personal than hosting some kind of death match in the home you grew up in? The place that's the stuff of *her* nightmares? I mean, she's willing to kill herself if we get this wrong. Why? Because she can't stand the idea of being misunderstood after she went to all this effort to be perceived by us. The house represents so much more than just a location. It's where she developed, where she turned from a girl to a villain, to a mastermind. To her, it would be the ultimate finale to be back there. And whatever goes down, when the world hears about what she's done... they'll remember her, they'll remember the house, they'll remember the story she told in her diary. Don't you see? The island was a cheap fame grab. *This* is how she solidifies her place in history. She'll have true crime documentaries, books, movies, all sorts of things about her. She'll seem so complex and cool to all those people who crave a really terrible story, fronted by a truly terrible woman. She'll be up there with the greats like Dahmer and Bundy. Except she will be superior, even, because she planned every detail down to her own ending. Which is yet to happen, of course, but she's building up to it. And whatever happens will be on her terms. That's why I think she will do it at her home, where she has all the control."

"You've been doing a lot of thinking about this, haven't you…"

"It's definitely been playing on my mind since she gave us the choice. But I'm only considering these thoughts based on the things you've been saying all along, Olivia. I think she believes that if anyone can truly decode her, it's us. And so she's been putting us through all of this to see if it was all worth it for this final game, a last opportunity for her to be immortalized by her own actions. Once news gets out about all of this, no one will ever allow her to fade into obscurity. And she is definitely narcissistic enough to host something like this in the house where she grew up, let's be real. This whole thing has been a study of who she is and what she's capable of, of her history and the becoming of the Gamemaster. I feel like her taking us to find her Aunt Teresa was to give the house some meaning in the story of her, and now she wants to come full circle and take us back there. In my mind it makes so much more sense than going back to the island. So if I had to guess… I think that's where she's drawing us to. Any thoughts?"

Olivia scratched at her head. "Well, that's a lot to take in."

"Except that I'm just working with what you've been saying all along, Olivia. I'm not really coming up with any ideas that you haven't already explored since we started on this case. I'm just piecing it together as the thoughts come to me." Brock sighed, running hand through his hair. "I feel kind of guilty."

"What? Why? What have you got to be guilty about?"

"I haven't been as present in this case as you have been. The cogs in your brain have been turning right from the start, and that's the only reason we have a clue about what might come next. I think you were right. At the core, this entire thing is about *her*. Every move she's made, every decision she's worked with…

it wasn't ever about us. It was about herself. I think I should've listened to you sooner. You've got the Gamemaster figured out even more than she's got herself figured out. She might not even realize just how much she's catered this to her own sick fantasies. She might believe she's out to get us, but in reality, she's out to put herself on a pedestal again. She wants to feed on the feeling she had last time. That's what you've been getting at for weeks, isn't it?"

"I mean, yes, that was my working theory..."

"Then can't it work to our advantage here? It seems like we've finally got a grip on understanding her. Can't we use all of this to make the final decision?"

Olivia considered it. "If everything that you're saying is true, then yes, I definitely think it makes sense for us to go back to the house. But that's relying on a lot of my thoughts being facts. And we can't be sure that they are. They're just musings about the most unpredictable woman we've ever been up against. I don't know if I'm confident enough in all of those thoughts for me to lay all of our plans on it. What if the Gamemaster has been manipulating us to think this way right from the start, just so that she can pull the rug out from underneath us when we show up in the wrong place? She seems like the kind of person who puts a lot of meaning into everything she does. What if she's been implanting false meaning into the things she's doing in order to trick us?"

"I mean, it's possible, but—"

"What if she wants to host at the island because it's where this all began, and she plans to end it there?"

"You could say the same about her house. It's where the Gamemaster was created, after all."

"Okay, that's true. But what if she wants to go back to the island to relive the biggest high of her career? What if she wants to go back to her glory days before she supposedly retires? And what if the thought of us not showing up there is enough for her to kill herself because somewhere along the way, she failed to get through to us?"

"Olivia... I think we both know deep down that she doesn't know how to give all of this up. Even if we make it through all of this and she is alive by the end of it... I don't know. I think she'll either carry on her tirade... or it'll all end here. For good. She won't stop until she's forced to. Do you catch my meaning?"

Olivia understood exactly what Brock was getting at, but it still made her stomach twist with anxiety to think that they were basing such a big decision on the theories she'd made about the Gamemaster over the last few weeks. She had faith in herself most of the time and she wanted to rely on herself now. She wanted to trust her gut and follow it to the end so that they could win. But the fact was, this was a life-or-death situation. If she was wrong, people would die. And that was something she was terrified to have on her conscience.

She looked to Brock for guidance.

"What if I'm wrong? What if all these assumptions I've made get people killed?"

Brock reached out to cup her cheek. "I have faith in you. Even if you don't feel certain right now... you have the most brilliant mind of anyone I know. I don't think you've made a mistake. The more I think about everything you came up with, the more likely it seems to me. But we can talk this through for hours and still be unsure. That's the thing about an ultimatum... it never feels good to make a decision. There are only two choices, and we have to pick one. We might as well have some theories to support our decision. If there's no logic to this, if she picked this at random... then we can only guess anyway. So either way, if we do happen to be wrong... then it's not our fault."

Olivia nodded silently. She knew they had to take the leap, one way or another. And she'd already made a subconscious choice before Brock had even spoken up about the theories.

She knew that they had to go to the house. It was what made the most sense. She wished she didn't have to wait to know whether they were right or not, but they still had to get back to the house and face whatever was there. And if they were wrong?

They'd watch everything go up in flames.

CHAPTER
TWENTY-FOUR

O LIVIA AND BROCK TOOK A NIGHT TO GET SOME REST IN a hotel ahead of their journey to the Gamemaster's house, but Olivia didn't sleep much. She tossed and turned for half of the night, her muscles tight and her stomach clenched. She couldn't escape the fear in her heart, knowing that her theories were the only thing standing between multiple people's lives and their deaths. By the time she got up the following morning and Brock began to drive them back to the house, she was a nervous wreck. It felt like all the strength had been sapped out of her body. She was worn down by weeks of overworking herself. Even now, at the final hurdle, it felt almost impossible to continue.

She wanted to curl into herself and let it all go. But Brock touched her arm gently, bringing her back down to earth.

"You can't let the Gamemaster see you like this," Brock reminded her. "This is what she wants. This is how she's figured out how to get under your skin."

"I know."

"She knows this decision will be tearing us apart, knowing that we could be condemning people to death. She wants us to suffer and throw us off our game before the finale. But if it's not about logic, then it's about chance. We work with what we know. If anything goes wrong, then it's not on us. It's not our fault."

Olivia knew he was right, and yet she still couldn't shake off the little voice in her head, telling her that she was about to fail everyone. Telling her that if she got this wrong then she was a terrible person, that she didn't deserve to have her career, her comfort, her life. The thought sank an invisible knife deep into her heart. Her own doubt was more painful than anything else that the Gamemaster had thrown at them so far. If she couldn't rely on herself and her own decisions, then she was nothing.

She wished for a moment that she wasn't who she was. She wished that she had an ordinary life where nothing bad almost never happened and there was always someone else to take the fall when something went wrong. She wished that by some chance, she and Brock had found their way to one another some other way, without all of the torture and pain they'd endured to get to where they were now. She wished for peace, beyond all else. Peace with Brock in Belle Grove, a quiet existence where nothing ever bothered them.

And then she pictured how boring that life would become after a while. She pictured never solving a case again. She pictured never getting to save someone's life, never getting to put her brain to good use, never sharing every win with Brock. And she knew deep down that without her job, she would never have found Brock. They were too different, despite some of the similarities they shared. Those similarities were tied up in their passion for their work. If they hadn't worked for the FBI, Olivia would be curled up somewhere with a book now and Brock would be flirting with beautiful women in bars in a big city. It was their job that made them so compatible in the first place, but without it, their paths just wouldn't have crossed, full stop. And that had to be one of the biggest tragedies she could ever imagine.

And she knew that a life without Brock wasn't for her. Not now that she'd had a taste of how good it could be with him at her side. She couldn't picture happiness without seeing him in her mind's eye. She hadn't truly known love until he came to her side. And before him, her job was all that she had really had.

And as hard as her job could be sometimes, as hard as the Gamemaster had pushed them, she didn't know how to live without the thrill of it all. She didn't like to admit that to herself very often—it made her feel bad for *enjoying* her work when it meant so many people suffering. But those people would suffer regardless, and they might never get justice without her. That's how she justified it to herself.

And without her today, everyone would die at the Gamemaster's hand regardless. If she and Brock just didn't bother to show up to either location, the Gamemaster would kill those people. By making the choice to show up at the house, she was giving those victims a chance. That's how she had to see it. She felt the knot in her stomach loosen a little. She was still afraid. She was still uncomfortable with the decision she'd had to make.

But now, she knew she was doing everything she could.

Brock hummed softly along with the radio as they drove. Olivia knew it was a nervous tic of his. He didn't want to talk about what they were about to face, and he couldn't stand the silence. If anyone saw them now, they might look like an ordinary couple on a road trip. But they were far from ordinary. And for a moment, that made Olivia smile.

She wouldn't have it any other way.

As they drew nearer the house, the sky clouded over and rain began to pour. It felt apt for their final faceoff with the Gamemaster.

Olivia put her hand on Brock's leg quietly, letting him know that they were in this thing together. It was a small comfort, but she thought it helped them both.

And all too soon, they were back at the house, driving up to the gate. But something felt different this time.

Something felt wrong.

The gate was wide open as they approached. The yellow police tape that had been there only days before when they reported Aunt Teresa's death was now flapping in the wind, leaving the entrance to the house open.

But it was what was in front of the house that made Olivia's heart turn cold.

Bodies. There were at least a dozen bodies strewn across the driveway and the unkempt grass. Police officers, it looked like. Olivia's heart seized. Clearly, the Gamemaster had come home to find them investigating and decided to wipe them out. Or she'd made someone do it for her. Olivia felt sick at the thought of Yara being forced to mow down so many people, bullets flying far too fast for anyone to get out alive.

But at least now they knew they were in the right place.

Brock parked the car and the pair of them sat in solemn silence, throats tight as they observed the chaos around them. Olivia knew they shouldn't be surprised by what the Gamemaster was willing to do at this point. She had never tried to disguise her lust for blood, after all. But seeing all those bodies laid out, knowing that an entire town would be in mourning for those men and women who had died for no good reason, hardened Olivia's heart. There wasn't a single redeemable quality inside the Gamemaster. She was a monster through and through.

And as if on cue, she stepped out of the house. It had been a few months since they had truly been face-to-face with Adeline Clarke, and she had clearly prepared for a grand appearance. It was an impression that would forever be etched in Olivia's mind. She remembered what Brock had said about Adeline immortalizing herself through the horror of everything she was doing. Olivia clenched her fists hard.

She would do everything she could to make sure that no one remembered who Adeline was.

On the surface, she looked pretty as a picture. She wore a sparkly pink ball gown and a plastic tiara as though she was dressed for a children's birthday party. She was grinning toothily, pink lipstick smeared across her mouth. She had strapped a rifle across her chest, ready for action at any given time. Olivia's breath hitched a little as she realized that the ballgown was splattered with blood. A permanent reminder of the lives lost that day.

"We have to go in there," Brock murmured. Olivia swallowed back her anger and fear.

"I know."

"I'm right here with you."

"I know that too."

Olivia and Brock stepped reluctantly out of the car. Adeline grinned and held up her hands in delight.

"You made it! And with time to spare!" she cried. "I'm so glad you could come. Welcome to the final task! Are you as hyped for this as I am?"

Olivia was shaking with rage at the sight of her. She wanted to end Adeline right there and then. The urge to shoot her and have it all done with was overwhelming. But she was certain that Adeline would have prepared for them trying to kill her before the games truly began. She was certain that doing so would kill the victims trapped inside the house. And now, with so many bodies laid out in front of the house already, she couldn't bear to be the reason that anyone else died.

"Lay down your weapons, please! I'm the only one allowed to have a gun in this house," Adeline said with a suspicious glare at the pair of them. "Don't make me mad before all the fun starts…"

Neither Olivia or Brock protested, laying down their pistols on the ground. It felt wrong to leave their only form of protection behind, but Olivia knew it was the only way. She stepped forward,

Brock falling into step with her as they headed back to the house. It felt like stepping into a haunted manor as a kid. Knowing that nothing good was inside, but doing it anyway because some other kid had dared them.

"Well, come on in!" Adeline said, ushering them with a wave of her arm. "I want to start the fun! I've laid out dinner for us. It might be a bit cold now, but there's wine..."

Olivia had no idea what strange game Adeline was trying to play with them, acting as if they were house guests, but she knew they had to go along with the madness. They were in her territory now. She knew they were all but powerless from the moment they stepped across the threshold.

The house looked mostly unchanged, save for another police officer lying dead in the entrance hall. Adeline stepped over the body without even looking properly, continuing to usher them to follow her.

"Come, come!"

Olivia felt like screaming, but she kept a lid on it all and followed her through the house. They made it to the grand dining room, where a table big enough for twenty people was set out for four. Olivia's stomach twisted. She was sure she could guess who the fourth guest would be.

"Here we are!" Adeline said with a flourish, gesturing to the dusty dining table. It was lit by candlelight and there was a roast dinner set out for them to eat. The food had clearly gone cold, the gravy congealed on the plate. "I call this The Last Supper! Consider it a little mini-game before the big event. Pre-gaming, if you will!"

She pulled out a chair and dragged Brock by his sleeve to sit down at the head of the table. Olivia didn't wait to be invited to sit, not wanting Adeline to touch her. She sat down beside Brock, knowing that Adeline was going to sit down directly opposite her. She didn't know how she would get through the meal pretending like everything was fine when it clearly wasn't. But she knew she had to endure, no matter how many buttons the Gamemaster attempted to push.

Adeline didn't seem to notice the tension in the room. She ran around, pouring glasses of wine for them and humming to herself.

"I promise the wine is safe to drink…I'll show you," she said, taking a swig right from the bottle. "It's a very old vintage. My dad bought it years and years ago. I think he bought it the year I was born when it was already super ancient. It was meant for sharing with me on my twenty-first birthday, but then he went and got himself killed. By me. Sad times. If only he could see me now. Do you think he'd be proud of me? I bet he never imagined me turning out this way… though I'm pretty sure he was no saint either. He might have appreciated everything I'm doing now. But then again, he was never around to see how brilliant I am. I don't think he deserves to take any credit for how I turned out to be."

Olivia said nothing, fixing her gaze on her plate and trying not to let anything bother her. She had to stay calm if she was going to make it through the day alive. But when she looked up again, Adeline was sitting opposite her, a determined look in her eyes. There was no trace of a smile on her face anymore.

"Drink," she growled. "This is a party. Act like it."

Olivia didn't hesitate to raise the wine to her lips, though some part of her was still concerned that she was being poisoned. She didn't put it past Adeline to poison herself just to get to them too. After everything, that seemed like an awful way to go. But she drank, and the deep red wine was good. She nodded to Adeline.

"It's delicious. A good choice. Thank you."

Adeline's smile returned, making her eyes wide and a little maniacal. Only in person was it obvious to Olivia just how crazy Adeline really was. Still, at least for the moment, she seemed to be on her side.

"I'm so glad you like it…oh, how could I forget! Our guest of honor! Yara, come in here!"

Olivia's heart dropped to her stomach as the doors opened and Yara stepped inside.

Except it wasn't really Yara anymore. The woman that slipped into the room was barely alive, like a ghost. Her footsteps hardly made a noise. Her face was gaunt and her eyes dead. She was pale and looked sickly with her hair plastered to her face. And when Olivia turned to see Brock's reaction, she saw a single tear fall down his face.

Yara said nothing as she joined them at the table, obediently picking up her wine as though she had been trained for this very moment. Adeline chuckled, putting her hand on Yara's sunken cheek.

"She's not had a drink in months, would you believe it? She took her sobriety so seriously. But I've trained her well. She knows exactly what I wanted her to do, and she did it without saying a word. See how it's done? Come on everyone, bottoms up! I can't expect you to be able to keep pace with Yara, though. It comes so naturally to her to get that wine down her gullet," Adeline said with a cruel laugh. Then she shoved Yara's face away roughly. Yara barely even reacted, keeping her eyes down. Red wine had spilled down her front like blood. Olivia couldn't help but stare at her.

The Gamemaster had truly broken her.

"A toast," Adeline said, her mouth twisted harshly. "To us… back together where we belong. I've waited a long time for this day and I'm so glad you made the right choice. I think this is the perfect place for our final reunion, don't you? Cheers!"

"Cheers," Olivia repeated, her voice barely a whisper. But she watched the moment when Yara raised the glass to her lips again and felt defeated. Would the Gamemaster ever stop? Did she want to break them the way she broke Yara?

It's going to be over soon. It will, Olivia promised herself. It was that promise that had kept her going these past weeks. But if it wasn't true, she didn't know how much more of this she could put herself through. It was emotional torture, and it would take a toll on them, just as it had on Yara.

Olivia didn't want to live to see herself end up like Yara.

Adeline sank back in her chair, cradling her glass of wine in her hand. She sighed, the smile leaving her face.

"You know... nothing has turned out like I expected it to," she said. "I planned for months to make this whole thing happen. I wanted to make you all suffer so much... but clearly, I haven't done a very good job. Because I look at Yara... and I know you haven't broken the way she has. Why is that, Olivia? Why aren't you broken yet? What do I have to do to make it happen?"

Olivia swallowed, planning her response cautiously.

"I guess I was waiting for the finale."

Adeline smirked. "Well, you're going to love it then. It'll be a real test of your strength I think. But I have to say, I still don't feel satisfied. I wanted to see fear in your eyes, and all I see is defiance. Because you're still fighting the good fight, aren't you? You think you can win this? Don't you know that it's all fun and games until it isn't? I can flip the switch whenever I like. Then you'll be sorry."

"We have suffered," Olivia said quietly. "We've lost so much—"

Adeline brought her fist down on the table, spilling Brock's glass all over the table.

"It's *not enough!*" she roared. It echoed painfully in the silent house. "I wanted pain. I wanted endless agony. I wanted to break the people who were sent to fix me, to tie me down and stop me from doing as I please. I needed that. You know why? Because I'm *bored.* And nothing is worse in this world than being so endlessly *bored. It's exhausting.* I need something more... something to keep me on my toes. I don't know when it stopped being fun... now it's just a chore. Like everything else."

Olivia kept her gaze on Adeline, worried about what she would do if she looked away for a moment. She had always considered her a dangerous woman, but now she was truly terrifying. Olivia felt that she was capable of anything.

Olivia realized she needed to keep Adeline engaged. She wanted the unexpected, the daring, the outlandish. Well, if that was what she needed, then she was going to have to provide. She sat up a little straighter, her eyes boring into Adeline's.

"Why?"

Adeline stared back, challenging Olivia's stamina. "Why what?"

"Why do you want us all to suffer? Why us? We didn't even know you before you came into our lives and started wreaking havoc. And now here we are."

Adeline frowned. "Because you were the best of the best. I thought that was obvious. I wanted a challenge. I wanted you to hunt me down to give me a reason to run. I wanted you to keep me on my toes."

"And haven't we done that much?" Olivia challenged. "We've survived everything you've thrown at us. We've solved every one of your puzzles. We haven't missed a single beat."

Adeline blinked in surprise, cocking her head to the side. "You know what? You're right. Maybe I'm not giving you enough credit for what you've done for me. But the problem is… where do I go from here, Olivia? How do I up the ante?" Adeline sunk further into her chair, looking like a sullen child who had just been scolded. "I'm running out of ideas. And I thought this was what I wanted. I thought I knew where I wanted to take the course of my life. But somewhere along the way… the things I wanted… they blurred."

Olivia nodded, listening to Adeline talk. She wanted an audience, so she'd give her one. Olivia could feel Yara and Brock sitting stiff, barely wanting to move and break the spell. Something in Adeline was unraveling right before their eyes.

"I'm so tired," Adeline whispered. "All this brilliance… I was caged for so long, and now that I'm free, I don't know how to use it. I have the energy and the drive, but my mind? It's just shut itself down. Locked me out. And the thing is, if you don't keep going, you fall behind. People have already moved on from what happened on the island. It's impossible to keep anyone's attention in this day and age. Everyone always wants more than they can have. And if you can't give it? You just fade into obscurity. No one is talking about what I did anymore. No one else has ever pulled off something so beautiful, so chaotic... and yet no one cares. And I can't step it up from there. There's nothing left for me to do... so I just keep trucking on, hoping that something will hit me soon. But I just feel so... empty. So finished."

"If you don't want this, you can always stop," Olivia murmured. Adeline blinked in surprise.

"...stop?"

"You don't have to do any of this," Olivia told her. "You know, some people use a brain like yours to do something good. Maybe the reason you don't have any satisfaction from this anymore is because you want a change of pace. You could do anything in this world, Adeline. If that doesn't excite you, I don't know what will."

Olivia watched Adeline's expression cycling through a thousand emotions. She looked like she couldn't quite comprehend the things she had heard. Olivia prayed that somehow she'd gotten through to her. That maybe she'd change her mind. She was just manic enough that it might work. And if it did, then maybe they'd all be able to walk free.

But life was never that simple. Adeline chuckled quietly to herself, a vacant look in her eyes.

"Maybe you're right," Adeline said, tipping her head back and draining the contents of her glass. But then her manic smile returned and she rose from the table. It was in that moment that Olivia knew nothing she had said had made it through. "But the party has to end at some point. And tonight is the night. I'll be ready for you soon. Sit tight. The games are about to begin."

CHAPTER
TWENTY-FIVE

O LIVIA, BROCK AND YARA FOLLOWED ADELINE THROUGH the house, the vastness of it filling Olivia with the prospect of thousands of possibilities. Would they be chased through the house like some horrific game of hide and seek? Would they be forced into a game of logic, a deadly chess match where the loser wound up dead? Olivia could imagine Adeline putting them through any one of those scenarios.

But she kept walking, taking them through the endless maze of rooms. When they finally reached the end of the house, Adeline opened the doors to their final destination.

The ballroom had clearly not been used in a long time. The windows were grubby and the floor was unpolished, scuffed with shoe marks and dents from furniture that had long been removed. In fact, there was very little in the room at all.

But it was still grand. There were gold etchings around the room and an ivory piano stood untouched in the corner. A beautiful crystal chandelier was hanging over the room. It felt so strange to be in the middle of the day and about to face something so terrifying, though rain pelted the windows and darkened the sky.

"It's time for the grand finale," Adeline cried out, opening her arms with a flourish to show them the ballroom. Now, her sparkling gown made some sort of sense. "And I couldn't have done it without some very important people. Yara, come to me."

Yara immediately shuffled forward like a zombie to be at Adeline's side, and Adeline threw a friendly arm around her shoulders. Olivia dug her nails into her palm, trying not to let her anger take over. Did Adeline really have to continue to make a spectacle of Yara after everything she had done to her? But, of course, she did. That was the whole reason she'd been involved in the first place.

"Yara here has been such a loyal pup. She's done everything I've told her to do. And I mean *everything*. She was the one who tied up dear Aunt Teresa and then stabbed her in the back while I watched. It took some convincing to make her do that, admittedly, but after I cut off her little toe, she was a lot more willing."

Yara's head was bowed so low that her chin was practically touching her chest. Olivia's throat was tight. She had known Yara's treatment would be terrible, but she had never imagined just how awful it would get for her. From the smile on Adeline's face, she pictured the very worst.

"What else has she gotten up to... oh yes, she was very helpful when the police came calling. She helped me take some of them down. And then she was there right at the beginning in St. Michael's, helping me hang dear Garrett Peabody from the ceiling of his store. But I guess that one wasn't so bad... considering that Garrett is still alive."

Olivia's jaw fell open as she watched Garrett appear from the back of the room. It was in fact he, and he was grinning as he walked over to them. Adeline began to applaud his arrival and he stopped short of them, bowing low, pride written all over his face.

"What the hell?" Brock asked. Adeline turned to him with a tut.

"Oh, Brock. You really should know the difference between a dead body and a wax figure. But I know I made it pretty convincing. That was the point. So that when the fire went off, all evidence of Garrett would simply melt away. Leaving him dead in the eyes of the law, and free to come and work for me. It's kind of funny… a vegan shopkeeper who cares so much about animal life, but it turns out he has a thirst for human blood."

"That makes me sound like some kind of vampire," Garrett laughed, shaking his head. "I've always found humans to be… intolerable. I prefer animals, hence my store. But I was looking to walk on the wilder side of life… and you, Adeline… you showed me how."

"You should see your faces!" Adeline cackled, pointing at Olivia and Brock. "You never saw that coming, did you? Don't worry, I've still got plenty of surprises in store."

"Was… was any of it real?" Brock asked, blinking in horror. "The tasks you set out for us… did any of it mean anything?"

"Of course it did! I might like playing mind games with you, but I was also curious how much I could push you and put you to the test. And you really did do a great job saving that little girl… I truly was glad that poor girl got to go home," Adeline said softly. But she quickly switched up again, her grin returning. "But I did have my fun watching you at the stadium… I've always wanted to put on such a performance, so I guess it was a little self-indulgent. At least you saved that poor janitor from being blown to bits by fireworks, right? And my assassin… how kind of you to show him mercy. It's a shame I won't do the same. He's next up on my list, once we're done here."

"You don't have to do this," Olivia pleaded. "This can all end here. We will finish up your tasks, but can't it all just end here."

Adeline chuckled. "Oh, Olivia. Sweet Olivia. You really thought you'd broken through to me back in the dining room, didn't you? You thought you had me reconsidering all my life choices. Well, here's a news flash, sweetheart. I don't regret a single thing. And I'm far from done. I had you convinced that you might change the course of my history, but I know exactly how I want to be remembered. The things that go down here today will be the stuff of legend. But I don't know if you'll be around to see it happen. I guess that depends how tonight goes."

"I know you've suffered," Olivia said. "Your life here was terrible. I'm sorry for everything you had to endure. But why would you want to make people feel the same way that you did? Don't you have any mercy?"

Adeline smirked, a twinkle in her eye. "You really shouldn't believe everything you see," she said. "Like, for example, the things written in a child's diary. I mean, really? Do I look like the kind of girl who has time to write a diary?"

Olivia blinked, not understanding what she was hearing. Adeline rolled her eyes.

"Do I have to spell it out for you? The diary was a fake. What you might call a red herring, I guess. See, that's another place where Yara really came in handy. While I was planning out all of this for you to enjoy, I didn't want her sitting idle. So I had her sit down and write an entire diary from my point of view. I mean, she was an actress. That's just lying on a TV screen, pretending to be someone you're not. I figured she could put all that creativity to good use elsewhere… and boy, did she do a good job. I think she really sold the lie, don't you?"

Olivia found herself well and truly speechless. Almost everything that she had based her theories on had come from that diary. And now, she was discovering that Adeline never had those experiences at all. It had been so real, so convincing, that Olivia couldn't quite believe that it wasn't true. She stared at Yara, but she wouldn't look at them.

"So why did you kill your Aunt Teresa? If none of it was true… then why? What did she do to deserve that."

"Oh, some of it was true. She did practically raise me… and the shows she used to watch really were boring as hell. But she did give me some gifts… she taught me chess and she was very clever. Not as clever as me, but not many people are. And she did have some strange ideas… she never did like leaving the house. But she didn't keep me locked in the house with her. I did whatever the hell I wanted. Do you really think I'd let someone control me that way? I escaped *federal prison*. She couldn't keep me caged if she tried," Adeline laughed.

"So why? Why did you kill her?" Brock pushed. Adeline considered the question for a second. Then she shrugged, completely nonchalant.

"I thought it would be fun, I guess. She was the last surviving member of my family… and what use did I have for her? She left her inheritance to some charity, and after I left home, she never spoke to me again. I was done with her, so I put her out of her misery. She should be grateful, really. She was just a waste of potential. All those brains and she was rotting away in front of the TV."

"So the only crime she committed was being a part of your family?" Olivia said through gritted teeth.

"I know. It's messed up. But while you've been trying to see a different side to me, looking for my complexities, I've been planning all of this. I hoped you'd read into it all too much, that you'd believe everything I was feeding you, because it means you underestimated me." Adeline took a step closer to Olivia, pointing the rifle she'd strapped around her at Olivia's head. "I'm not that complicated, girlie. All you need to know about me is that I want to hurt people. Not because they hurt me, but because I enjoy it. I'm just here to have a good time, to play some games, and to win.

And I guess I've managed that, because seeing the look on your faces just now? Nothing has ever been sweeter."

Olivia swallowed back her disappointment, staring down the gun. She thought she had begun to understand the Gamemaster, but it had all been another test. She'd been wrong about so much. She'd allowed Adeline to spoon feed her lie after lie.

And she'd eaten it up willingly.

"You know what? I'm going to miss you guys," Adeline said, pouting her lip. "These last few weeks I feel like we've gotten so close… we really had a rapport going. But unfortunately it can't continue. It's not healthy for any of us. And I don't like getting attached."

Adeline lowered the gun, and Olivia sighed. She hadn't felt as though she was about to shoot—it would be far too simple for her to kill them that way. No, whatever the Gamemaster had planned was going to be much more detailed.

"I'm just playing with you," Adeline said, walking away. "I wouldn't want you to miss the finale. Shall we begin?"

"Just tell us what to do," Olivia said firmly. Adeline turned back to her with a twinkle in her eyes.

"Oh, you don't need to do anything. At least not for now. To start off the show with a bang, I figured I'd have you in the audience. Take three steps back and three away from each other. I don't want any funny business from either of you."

Olivia and Brock did as they were told. Olivia's heart was racing so hard that she felt sick. Adeline gave them a curt nod, satisfied by their obedience.

"And now for something that actually goes bang… here, Yara, take this."

Adeline shoved a pistol into Yara's hands. She looked shocked to be holding something with so much power in her hands. Olivia wondered why she didn't just turn and shoot the Gamemaster, but she seemed to be frozen to the spot.

"Good girl," Adeline murmured. "I've trained you well. And I've got a surprise for you. Someone you haven't seen for a long time. I figured you'd like a final reunion."

What does that mean? Olivia wondered. And that's when Garrett returned to the room, holding someone in his grip. It was a woman, her mascara running down her face and her bleached blonde hair tousled. She had big doe eyes that were filled with fear. Whoever it was seemed to upset Yara because she let out a low moan, shaking her head in horror.

"That's Yara's best friend, Kiera," Brock choked out. He was about to run to help her, but Olivia shook her head.

"Don't. She'll kill us all if you move, you know she will," Olivia warned him. "We have to figure out what's going on here."

"She's going to make Yara kill her."

"Don't spoil the surprise!" Adeline laughed. "And now you know what all of our target practice has been in preparation for, Yara. This isn't Olivia and Brock's final test. It's yours."

Olivia held her breath as Garrett forced Kiera to stand opposite Yara. She was trembling and sobbing, her eyes trained on Yara.

"Yara, sweetie... w-what happened to you?"

"I changed," Yara said robotically, her eyes trained on her former friend. Adeline smirked, satisfied with her response. There was no faking the dead look in Yara's eyes. It looked as though she had truly been defeated by Adeline's antics.

"No... no, you don't need to do this," Kiera sobbed. "Do you really want the last thing I see to be your gun pointing in my face?"

Yara raised the gun until it was level with Kiera's forehead. She didn't even blink. Her hands didn't tremble. She knew exactly what she was going to do, and she wasn't afraid to do it. Kiera cowered, sobbing.

"Yara, please don't do this," Olivia blurted out. "It'll never end. She's never going to let you go. Is this how you want to live?"

Yara turned the gun on Olivia, unblinking.

"I know what I'm doing," she said. She looked Olivia up and down. "And if you say another word, I'll kill you too."

Olivia felt her blood turn to ice. Up until that point, she hadn't been certain that Yara would go through with it. But this time felt different. She didn't have a gun to her own head, but she may as well have. Yara was so under Adeline's spell that she was willing to do anything she was told.

Yara pointed the gun at Brock next, watching his eyes turn to stone. She scoffed at him.

"And you're not worth my bullet."

Brock's hard exterior crumbled. "Who are you?"

"Everything you should want to be," Yara said coldly. And then her gun was back on her best friend. Kiera screamed.

"Yara, no!"

Yara smiled.

And pointed the pistol up.

Before Olivia could register what Yara was doing, the gun fired. Straight into the fixture supporting the chandelier. There was a strangled cry from Adeline as the chandelier fell, too fast for her to scramble away.

The entire thing came crashing down on top of the Gamemaster and Garrett. Olivia saw Kiera throw herself to the ground as the chandelier shattered, glass-like knives scattering around the room. Olivia shielded her face at the last moment, feeling shards scutter past her, hearing the surprised gasps turn into agonized shrieks.

And then there was silence.

Olivia waited for her heart to slow, but it didn't. And when she uncovered her face, Yara was the only one left standing, observing the metal structure pinning Adeline down.

Slowly, cautiously, Olivia and Brock moved to Yara's side. Olivia didn't know what she might do—she had them all fooled until the last moment. But when she noticed Olivia beside her, she offered the pistol to her calmly. With shaking hands, Olivia took the weapon away from her.

There was a quiet groan from beneath the chandelier. Garrett was out cold, maybe even dead. Blood pulsed from a wound on the side of his head.

But Adeline was still alive. For now. Her skin had been pierced so many times with glass shards that it looked like spikes protruded from her skin. The huge chandelier had fallen thunderously, breaking both legs and cutting deep gashes. Her bones looked misshapen, pinned underneath the metal structure that had once held up the chandelier, where a dark pool of blood expanded. As Olivia, Brock, and Yara moved closer, a gurgling laugh escaped Adeline's bloodied lips.

"The student becomes the master," she laughed. "But I had so much left to teach you."

"You couldn't teach me anything. I already knew suffering before you. You just made me stay in it," Yara said quietly.

Adeline reached out with trembling fingers. "You were supposed to be mine. My best creation. You were supposed to follow me all the way."

"And I did," Yara said. "All the way to the end of you. Game over, Adeline."

A single tear began to trickle down Adeline's cheek. "What about my legacy? What about everything we worked for?"

Yara's eyelids looked heavy with grief as she bent down beside Adeline's ruined body. She picked up a shard of glass with one hand and took hold of Adeline's hand with the other.

"That will die with you. And with me."

And without a trace of emotion or sentiment, Yara quickly sliced Adeline's throat with cold, calculated precision.

Olivia saw something like pleading in Adeline's final glance at Yara. And then she went still, her eyes glassy.

She was gone.

Yara stood up, letting Adeline's hand drop to the floor. Olivia didn't know what to say or what to do next. Yara was still a wanted woman. She had just proved how dangerous she could be, too.

But when Yara slowly turned to them again, she held out her bony wrists to Olivia.

"You should cuff me," she said. "End this for good."

Her wrists were so thin now that Olivia doubted cuffs would even work on her. She shook her head at Yara slowly.

"Yara…"

"I meant what I said," she insisted. "This is the end of the line. For Adeline and for me. Cuff me. It's time to put all of this to rest."

It was Brock who stepped forward to do it. Yara searched Brock's face as he cuffed her, but he refused to look her in the eye. Even after everything, he couldn't even look at her.

And Olivia understood.

Because the moment Adeline died, Yara had become the most evil thing left in the room.

CHAPTER TWENTY-SIX

THERE WAS A LOT TO UNCOVER AFTER ADELINE DIED. Olivia and Brock secured the rest of the house, finding in the process that Adeline had a whole room full of other victims, tied up and ready to go for the big finale that she had originally planned. One of them told Olivia that Adeline had planned to make them all play a game of Russian Roulette, Olivia and Brock included. Olivia couldn't help feeling endless relief. Yara's actions back at the ballroom had saved so many people, whether she was aware of it or not. And now, because of her, Olivia and Brock had survived the final game that Adeline would ever force them to play.

When Olivia and Brock finally managed to call for backup, there was a lengthy process to go through with the other FBI agents. They had to explain everything they'd been through, how the Gamemaster had been putting them through their paces for the last few weeks. By the time they explained what had happened inside Adeline's family home, Olivia could tell that their story had left many people stunned.

But all she felt was numbness while she talked about what they'd been through. It made her feel safer, hiding behind words that didn't sound real coming out of her mouth. She could almost pretend like it had happened to someone else that way. But every time she concentrated too hard on her surroundings, she couldn't help coming back to reality. The bloodied chandelier under which Adeline lay dead was now surrounded by agents collecting evidence. Kiera was standing shivering as she gave her testimony.

And then there was Yara. She hadn't moved since she had been cuffed and now sat on the ground, her knees tucked up to her chin protectively. Brock had been keeping his distance, making himself busy anywhere else that he could. Olivia kept an eye on her, though. As much as she knew that Yara wasn't a good person, she also knew that she'd been molded that way by very capable hands. She'd been tortured and manipulated for so long now that she was unrecognizable as the person she had been before. Back then, she hadn't deserved to get mixed up in something so awful. And now? She'd made her final choice. She'd killed the Gamemaster, knowing it was the only way to save what was left of her own soul and to end the cycle for good. She had done the right thing for everyone in the end. That had to be worth something.

There was a shred of good left inside Yara.

She didn't protest as she was taken away. Kiera tried to talk to her as she was escorted out, but Yara kept her head down, refusing to engage with anyone. Olivia understood to an extent. She didn't want sympathy or kindness. She wanted to accept what she had done and do her time for it. Another sign of the goodness left inside her. It was just about the only sign of humanity left in the broken woman who left the house that day.

When Olivia and Brock were allowed to leave, they headed straight home to Belle Grove. There was nothing to be said and nothing left to do. They collapsed into bed together and held one another tightly, glad to be free, glad that the nightmare was finally over.

But it was a few days later when they finally managed to broach the subject of Yara once again. Brock stared at Olivia as she revealed what she wanted to do.

"Why on earth would you want to go and visit her?"

"I feel like I want to see her one final time. To let her know that I'm grateful that she did what she did," Olivia said. "More people would have died if she hadn't done it."

"And what about the people who died because of her already?"

"They died because of the Gamemaster, for the most part. She played her part too, but we both know she would never have done those things by choice. She was backed into a corner—"

"Please don't defend her, Olivia. Can't we just be glad that the best outcome came out of this? She's back where she belongs… don't tell me you want to bail her out too?"

"Brock, please. You're refusing to see what I mean. I know we don't owe her anything. I know that she's done bad things. But she saved lives back at Adeline's home. She saved *our* lives. God knows what Adeline had planned for us after Yara's 'test.' I'm not forgiving her. I just want some closure."

Brock shook his head. "I don't understand that. Is it not over already? Was seeing her carted off to prison not enough closure for you?"

"Not really, if I'm honest. I just want to close this chapter in my own way. I understand if you don't want to come with me. And if you tell me that you don't want me to go, I won't. But I want to see her one final time, if I can."

Brock sighed, running a hand through his hair. He shook his head.

"Look, I can't come with you. I just can't face it. But if you want to say goodbye, then I don't have a problem with you doing that. You'll just have to go alone. And leave me out of whatever you say to her. I don't want anything to do with her."

Olivia nodded, though she could see the pain in Brock's eyes. The whole thing had been dragged out for so long now that it felt like Brock would always be plagued by what his friend had done. She would respect what he wanted—if he said he was done with Yara, then that was his choice—but she knew even before she went to see Yara that he would be the first name on Yara's tongue.

Olivia visited as soon as she was able to, heading to the visiting area to wait for Yara. Yara joined her at the window, picking up the phone on the other side.

"You look better," Olivia told her. Yara nodded, unsmiling.

"I guess so. I've been eating a little. I was getting used to starving… but I'm still not well. Not that I'm asking for any sympathy. That would be ridiculous." She paused, her eyes drifting to the empty space behind Olivia. "Brock didn't join you?"

Olivia bit her lip. "No… I'm sorry."

"Why are you sorry? I understand completely," Yara said, her voice devoid of any emotion at all. When Olivia looked at her now, there was no life at all in her eyes. "He doesn't want to come and visit a killer. Not many people do. I wouldn't, if the shoe was on the other foot."

"You… you went through a lot."

"So do plenty of people. They don't do the things I did to stay alive. And for what?" Yara asked bluntly. Her eyes met Olivia's as she pressed her palm against the glass. "Listen to me, Olivia. This is coming from the heart. Don't waste a second feeling sorry for me."

"I just—"

"No. Let me finish. Don't do this to yourself. Don't do it to Brock. You went through hell and back. I watched it happen, remember? I could have done more, but I didn't. I was trying to save my own skin. But somewhere along the way… I realized that

I didn't know why I was doing it anymore. And I vowed to myself that whenever I got the chance, I would make things right. Even if it meant the end of my own life, or my freedom. I knew what I was willing to do when I took the gun from Adeline. I knew I just had to fool her for a little longer." She offered a sad smile. "I guess I always was an actress. And this was the role of a lifetime. I guess I took my method acting a little too seriously." She barked a quick laugh. "I bet someone's writing that about me in the tabloids now. I'm more famous now than I ever was as an actress." She swallowed, her eyes filling with tears. "I never wanted things to be this way. There was a time when I believed I wasn't capable of ever hurting a person. I never once considered being violent toward someone. It just didn't sit right with me. But the second my life was threatened… I became such a monster. I look in the mirror now and I don't even know who I am. I'm… I'm starting to even forget the person I was. I can't picture myself in my mind. And it scares me half to death. If I could turn back time… I would rather die than do the things that I did. I wouldn't even consider putting people through those things again."

"I know."

Yara's eyes were wide and earnest. "I want you to know… I never would've killed you, or Brock. Even way back when I was still fighting for myself. When I killed the others… it was easier. I didn't know them. I could convince myself that the worth of my own life outweighed theirs. I know better now, of course. But you were some of the best friends I ever had, which is a sad statement to make. You did things for me that no one else would. You tried to save me. And I threw that back in your faces."

Olivia swallowed, feeling a lump resting in her throat. "It's good to hear you say that."

"And do you believe me?" Yara asked, a hint of desperation present in her tone. "That's all I want. To know that you believe I would never have hurt you."

"I believe you. I promise."

Yara sat back in her chair, relief visible on her face. "Good. That's the best I could've ever hoped for after what I did. And for what it's worth, I'm so sorry. Endlessly sorry."

"I believe that too."

They sat looking at one another for a few moments, the silence heavy between them. Yara sniffed.

"I… I wrote some things down. A lot of things, actually. An account of everything that happened. I want you to give it to Brock. I'll have it mailed to you. If he doesn't read it, that's okay. But I wanted him to have the option to get inside my head. To let him know that I didn't do any of it willingly. To let him know that I live with my regrets every day. And I want him to know… that I love him. He meant so much to me. He should know that much."

Olivia swallowed. "I'll take it… but I can't promise that he'll read it. He… he doesn't really want to know."

Yara lowered her eyes. "I know. I expected nothing less. But maybe somewhere down the line… he'll change his mind. And then he can find me between the pages."

"Maybe he'll come visit, when he's ready," Olivia said, but there was no conviction to her words. Yara knew that too. She shrugged.

"At least I can say that I tried. You should get home to him now, Olivia. And as someone that cares about you… don't try and come back here. Please. I think it's best that you leave me in the past now."

Olivia nodded. She'd got what she came for. Yara looked almost sad as Olivia waggled her fingers to her one final time. She waved back, their final goodbye a wordless one. Then Olivia got up and walked away.

She had no idea that by morning, Yara would be dead.

CHAPTER
TWENTY-SEVEN

THE REPORT OF YARA'S DEATH HIT THE NEWS BEFORE
Olivia and Brock even received a call about it. Olivia
woke in the middle of the night to a news alert about it,
and she was forced to wake Brock and tell him the news.

She had killed herself in her cell. Now that Olivia thought
back to her conversation with Yara, she knew she should've seen
the signs of what was coming. Warning Olivia not to return,
writing down the story of what had happened to her under the
Gamemaster's thumb, the dead look behind her eyes. As Olivia
held Brock close, guilt squeezed her heart. But she knew deep
down that she couldn't have done anything to save Yara.

She was too far gone.

Brock didn't cry at first. They quietly held one another until the early hours of the morning before Brock went to sleep. Only then did Olivia read through the articles, her throat tight as she discovered what had happened to Yara.

She'd managed to hang herself, but not before she had written a lengthy suicide note. The note detailed the extent of her crimes and her guilt. She had decided to leave her significant fortune to the families of the victims she had affected and the ones still alive after the Gamemaster's games—Bethany and her family, the janitor from the stadium, and Kiera.

She requested that there would be no funeral for her.

A few days passed in near silence. Olivia knew that Brock was hurting, but she couldn't seem to reach him. He walked around like a zombie, sort of like how Yara had been in her final days. Olivia wanted to tell him things that might comfort him—that Yara loved him, that she had written an account for him, that she was sorry. But she knew none of those things would mean all that much to him. He didn't care that she was sorry. He cared that she was gone, though he was unlikely to ever admit that now. Not after everything.

Five days later, Olivia returned from the store to find Brock crying on the sofa. She immediately dropped her groceries bag and ran to his side, enveloping him in her arms and allowing him to cry on her shoulder. His body shuddered, and Olivia knew he was letting out months' worth of hurt and confusion. He had been so determined to keep it locked away, and now that the floodgates were open, she knew he would struggle for a long time to close them again. But it was for the best. She wanted him to let it go so that, someday, they might be able to move on with their lives.

"I shouldn't be crying for her," Brock said eventually, taking a shuddering breath to try and calm himself. "Not after the things that she did."

"You and I both know that grief is more complicated than that, Brock. You have nothing to feel guilty about."

"But she hurt so many people. Me included."

"She did. But before all of this… You shared a lot of good memories. Those don't get erased by the bad ones. You're mourning the person she was when you loved and understood her. And you're sad that it all had to come to this. That's not strange, you know. You're completely entitled to those feelings."

Brock considered her words for a moment and then he nodded. He wiped at his eyes, letting out a frustrated noise.

"I'm sorry."

"Don't be. It's good to let it out."

"It's just… I never expected it to feel this way. And I never pictured her doing this to herself. She never would've a year ago. She had a tough time with life sometimes… but she used to be happy. She used to find so much to live for. That's why I liked her so much. She was just full of love and energy and positivity."

"I know. I missed that version of her as well."

Brock swallowed back a sob, not looking Olivia in the eye.

"I never… I never got to say goodbye properly. And I wish now… I guess if I had known it was the last time I was ever going to speak to her, to see her… I would've said *something*. I don't know what, but I would've just… spoken to her."

"You were angry, and you had every right to be. No one blamed you for keeping your distance. She understood why. She didn't expect anything from you, and you didn't owe it to her."

"But now I'll never… I'll never get to say goodbye. There isn't even going to be a funeral. I missed my chance."

Olivia's heart ached for Brock. She slipped her hand into his.

"You don't need a coffin and a church to have a funeral. We can have one here. And we can say goodbye in the privacy of our home. No one needs to know. It might even be better this way."

Brock finally looked at Olivia, his eyes shining with unshed tears.

"You know… I think you understand me in a way no one else ever can. You know exactly what's on my mind, don't you? The guilt. The fear of what other people will think of me mourning the woman who caused so much destruction. But you still know how to make it better."

"Of course I do, Brock. I love you," Olivia murmured. "I know you inside out. I know you on a level I've never wanted to know anyone else on. And I see through you. Even when you're putting up a front, I know what you're thinking and what you need. But that's the whole point of this… of you and me. We can help each other when we don't really know how to help ourselves."

Brock sniffed, squeezing her hand. "I love you more than I can ever describe."

"I love you too. So much."

They hugged each other for a long time. When they parted again, Brock looked a little better. His hand slipped into Olivia's again.

"Do you think… do you think things will ever be okay again? Right now, it feels like we'll never get our happiness back."

"We will. But I think it'll take time," Olivia said. "We went through so much. Things most people never have to even consider. It's natural for us to need some time to recover."

"And when we do… we won't let anyone break us ever again, right? Because now… I don't want to trust anyone again. No one but you."

Olivia smiled sadly. "That'll change again with time. But I'm not going anywhere. And I promise that no matter what life throws at us, you will always be able to trust me. You'll never have to wonder if I'm capable of betraying you. I'd rather die than hurt you the way others have."

"Same here," Brock said, leaning his forehead against hers. "Man, that's corny."

Olivia laughed and she caught a glimpse of Brock's famous smile. When he pressed his lips gently to hers, she felt her whole chest fill with warmth. She'd missed his kiss. She'd missed these moments where it was just the two of them with no dark clouds hanging over them. The skies were clearer now. Even if just for a while, everything was going to be okay.

"Do you think things will be calmer now?" Brock whispered. Olivia shrugged.

"Who knows. Everything has changed. For once … I have no idea what the future holds."

"Maybe that's not such a bad thing. Maybe for once, there's a good surprise on the horizon."

"Let's hope so. We've had enough bad ones to last a lifetime."

"Maybe we just need to make our own destiny," Brock said with a wry smile. "What do you want to do next?"

Olivia smiled. "I want to focus on you and me. For the rest of time."

Brock smiled back. "I think that's something I can manage."

EPILOGUE

I T TOOK A LITTLE WHILE FOR OLIVIA AND BROCK TO SETTLE
back into ordinary life. Olivia had known that there would
be no easy path back to normality, but she was glad that she
had Brock to take the journey with her.

They eased back into work, taking the opportunity to work
on some easier cases for a while when they were offered to them.
They kept to themselves and their family, feeling alone in their
issues. And quietly, they mourned what they had lost.

But the heaviness in Olivia's heart began to lift, and she
noticed that Brock was beginning to feel the same. While it never
went away entirely, they both found themselves able to find happy
moments here and there. Days passed without tears and pain,
replaced instead by laughter and inside jokes and sun parting the
clouds in their lives. It made the previously unbearable time feel

like a nightmare that was fading away. Olivia watched the light return to Brock's eyes, and she felt so glad. She had been worried she might not see it again.

And then they decided that what they really needed was a vacation. Since their disastrous ski lodge trip, they hadn't really taken another opportunity to get away, but Olivia knew that they could both use time away from Belle Grove and the memories they had built there. Reality could be harsh, and she was more than happy to escape it for a while.

So she and Brock packed their suitcases and headed out to sunny Barcelona. Olivia hadn't spent much time in Europe before, but she found herself enamored with the city. The heat was stifling, but it didn't stop her from wanting to explore Park Guell, only ducking inside for a day to look around the Picasso museum. They spent a couple of days drinking cocktails on the beach, and then they visited the Basilica de la Sagrada Familia, marveling at the scale of the project in front of them.

"It's amazing… all these years and it still isn't finished," Brock said, staring up at the imposing building. Olivia nodded.

"For sure. But then again, everything is a work in progress…"

"Wow. That's so deep, Olivia. You should be a philosopher."

Olivia elbowed him, rolling her eyes with a smile as Brock laughed at her. She didn't care about the teasing. She felt drunk on the entire experience. This was everything she had ever wanted. Having fun with the love of her life, enjoying the sunshine and the culture. It was more than she could have wished for.

That evening, Brock told Olivia to dress up a little—he was taking her for drinks in the city. Olivia had a sneaking suspicion that something was about to happen, so she put on her favorite black dress, even swapping her sensible tennis shoes for a pair of pumps with small heels. She found an old red lipstick in her purse and put some on. It was a bit out of her comfort zone, but if tonight was going to be as special as she thought it was, then, she knew it would be worth it. She wanted Brock to remember the way she looked that night.

And she knew she'd remember every detail of him too. The cheeky smile on his handsome face, the crisp blue shirt he wore and the neatly pressed slacks. The way his eyes shone as he took her in, shaking his head in disbelief.

"Damn, Olivia. You get more and more beautiful every time I look at you," he murmured, pulling her in by her waist. She brushed her lips gently against his.

"I wanted to look good for tonight," she said, leaving something unspoken between them. They both knew what the night was going to be, but Olivia didn't mind. She didn't need to be surprised. In fact, the anticipation only made her more thrilled for what was about to happen. She just wanted to know how it would all pan out.

Brock took them to the Magic Fountain of Montjuic. As their taxi pulled up outside the fountain, the light show was just about to begin. Brock offered Olivia a sweet, warm smile and took her hand, leading her to get the best view of the majestic show.

But Olivia wasn't looking at the lights or the water. She only had eyes for him. And as music swelled around them, captivating the people standing close by, she waited for the moment she knew was coming. The moment where he would get down on one knee and promise himself to her forever.

And he did.

He was smiling as he took a box out of his jacket and sunk down on one knee. Olivia gripped his free hand, her throat tight as she held back tears of happiness. She'd been proposed to before, but it had been nothing like this. No beautiful venue, no lights show, no beautiful diamond ring shining in the moonlight.

No Brock.

"Olivia," he breathed, his voice accompanied only by the Spanish music in the background. "I've waited so long to do this, but I wanted to wait for the perfect time. The moment had to be *just right*. You deserve the most beautiful proposal because after everything you've been through… I want you to have a moment of magic to look back on. A moment just for the two of us."

Olivia smiled encouragingly, nodding for him to continue. Brock smiled back, shaking his head in disbelief.

"I count my blessings every single day with you, Olivia. I never pictured myself settling down and falling in love. I always thought I'd fly solo and love it that way. But I can't picture a day without you at my side, and I don't want to. You came into my life because I needed you, whether I knew it or not. And I don't know what's in it for you—marrying a big goofball like me—but I would consider it an honor to spend the rest of my life with the most beautiful, most caring, most intelligent woman I've ever met. Nothing can top this for me, Olivia. If you say yes… then just know that you've completed me in every possible way. I don't need anything more. Just this… what we have now, forever. But that said, I'll live the rest of my days trying to please you, trying to show you the world, trying to give you everything you've ever wanted or needed. So Olivia Knight… will you marry me? Will you be my wife?"

Olivia didn't answer right away. She took a second to savor the moment, her heart fluttering like butterfly wings in her chest. She had known so much darkness in her life, especially in recent years. But now here Brock was, presenting himself to her, a shining beacon through the dark night. How could she even consider saying no when he was offering her everything she had ever craved?

"Of course I will," she whispered. Brock grinned.

"Thank goodness."

Olivia laughed as Brock slipped the ring onto her finger. It was a perfect fit. It brought a tear to her eyes, seeing the ring resting perfectly on her hand. Brock stood up and swept her into his arms, twirling her around. She laughed again, her heart soaring as she spun around. She had a feeling of *deja vu*, the joy of spinning around on a playground as a kid. And that was how Brock had always made her feel—he reminded her not to take life too seriously, to tap into her childhood self again, to experience joy the way she did when she was a kid who didn't understand how cruel life could be. Now, the pair of them could feel that way forever.

As the show came to its big finale, colored water spurting toward the sky like fireworks, Brock wrapped his arms around her and kissed her. It was like something out of a movie, but ten times better. Right there, right then, it was just the two of them against the world. And Olivia knew that now, no matter what came their way, they would be able to face it.

Together.

AUTHOR'S NOTE

Thank you for reading FATAL LIES, the exciting conclusion to Season Two in the Olivia Knight FBI Series! We hope you enjoyed the story and the epilogue, which was crafted especially for you, our cherished reader. Olivia and Brock have faced countless harrowing moments together, and they deserved every bit of that special moment. We hope it left you feeling that they haven't just survived their ordeals but have grown stronger because of them.

If you've been following our newsletter, you know we're taking a break from the Olivia Knight series to plan the perfect next chapter for Olivia and Brock. This break also allows us to focus on our exciting new project, Serenity Springs. This new series is a passion project inspired by your insightful emails and enthusiastic feedback. We wanted to honor YOU by creating something truly special. If you haven't already experienced THE GIRL IN THE SPRINGS, we hope you will soon!

As indie writers, we rely heavily on the support and feedback from readers like you. If you enjoyed FATAL LIES, please consider leaving a review. Your reviews make a significant difference, helping us reach more readers without a big marketing budget or a massive following.

Thank you for your immense support for the Olivia Knight series. We hope you'll join us in Serenity Springs, where more adventures and mysteries await.

By the way, if you find any typos, have suggestions, or just simply want to reach out to us, feel free to email us at egray@ellegraybooks.com

Your writer friends,
Elle Gray & K.S. Gray

CONNECT WITH ELLE GRAY

Loved the book? Don't miss out on future reads! Join my newsletter and receive updates on my latest releases, insider content, and exclusive promos. Plus, as a thank you for joining, you'll get a FREE copy of my book Deadly Pursuit!

Deadly Pursuit follows the story of Paxton Arrington, a police officer in Seattle who uncovers corruption within his own precinct. With his career and reputation on the line, he enlists the help of his FBI friend Blake Wilder to bring down the corrupt Strike Team. But the stakes are high, and Paxton must decide whether he's willing to risk everything to do the right thing.

Claiming your freebie is easy! Visit
https://dl.bookfunnel.com/513mluk159
and sign up with your email!

Want more ways to stay connected? Follow me on Facebook and Instagram or sign up for text notifications by texting "blake" to 844-552-1368. Thanks for your support and happy reading!

ALSO BY
ELLE GRAY

Blake Wilder FBI Mystery Thrillers

Book One - *The 7 She Saw*
Book Two - *A Perfect Wife*
Book Three - *Her Perfect Crime*
Book Four - *The Chosen Girls*
Book Five - *The Secret She Kept*
Book Six - *The Lost Girls*
Book Seven - *The Lost Sister*
Book Eight - *The Missing Woman*
Book Nine - *Night at the Asylum*
Book Ten - *A Time to Die*
Book Eleven - *The House on the Hill*
Book Twelve - *The Missing Girls*
Book Thirteen - *No More Lies*
Book Fourteen - *The Unlucky Girl*
Book Fifteen - *The Heist*
Book Sixteen - *The Hit List*
Book Seventeen - *The Missing Daughter*
Book Eighteen - *The Silent Threat*
Book Nineteen - *A Code to Kill*
Book Twenty - *Watching Her*
Book Twenty-One - *The Inmate's Secret*
Book Twenty-Two - *A Motive to Kill*
Book Twenty-Three - *The Kept Girls*

A Pax Arrington Mystery

Free Prequel - Deadly Pursuit
Book One - I See You
Book Two - Her Last Call
Book Three - Woman In The Water
Book Four- A Wife's Secret

Storyville FBI Mystery Thrillers

Book One - The Chosen Girl
Book Two - The Murder in the Mist
Book Three - Whispers of the Dead
Book Four - Secrets of the Unseen
Book Five - The Way Back Home

A Sweetwater Falls Mystery

Book One - New Girl in the Falls
Book Two - Missing in the Falls
Book Three - The Girls in the Falls
Book Four - Memories of the Falls
Book Five - Shadows of the Falls
Book Six - The Lies in the Falls
Book Seven - Forbidden in the Falls
Book Eight - Silenced in the Falls
Book Nine - Summer in the Falls

ALSO BY
ELLE GRAY | K.S. GRAY

Olivia Knight FBI Mystery Thrillers

Book One - New Girl in Town

Book Two - The Murders on Beacon Hill

Book Three - The Woman Behind the Door

Book Four - Love, Lies, and Suicide

Book Five - Murder on the Astoria

Book Six - The Locked Box

Book Seven - The Good Daughter

Book Eight - The Perfect Getaway

Book Nine - Behind Closed Doors

Book Ten - Fatal Games

Book Eleven - Into the Night

Book Twelve - The Housewife

Book Thirteen - Whispers at the Reunion

Book Fourteen - Fatal Lies

A Serenity Springs Mystery Series

Book One - The Girl in the Springs

Book Two - The Maid of Honor

ALSO BY
ELLE GRAY | JAMES HOLT